Mahjong

Is

Murder

Lou Fletcher

Cover Design: Kandy Witte
Photographer: Bob Witte
Cover Model: Jane Foley Biddinger

Copyright © 2017 Witt's End Press
All rights reserved.
ISBN:0-9910073-9
ISBN-13:978-0-9910073-7-0

ACKNOWLEDGMENTS

I wish to express my sincere gratitude to my family, my fellow writers of the Ohio Valley Writers Network and the Cincinnati Writers' Project for encouragement, support and critical feedback. I also want to thank my fellow mahjong players, Jane Biddinger, Bonnie May, Peggy Potts and Dawn Trammel, who provided the inspiration – and the laughs – for the book. It really did take a village!

For Noah

ONE

"I'm dead," Tippi Mulgrew groaned.

The last tile she'd needed to stay in the game had been thrown. She stood and stretched her arms above her six-foot frame.

Gert Schwab kept one eye on her tiles and the other on her friend who pressed her elbows against the sides of her waist and twisted as far as she could to the right, to the left, then back again. She held up a hand to halt play so she could watch Tippi thrust out her arms then bend at the waist in a futile attempt to touch the toes of her flowered Converse hi-tops.

"Feelin' the burn, Jane?" Gert said referring to their younger days in front of the television exercising—Gert mentally inserted air quotes around that word— to a Jane Fonda workout tape.

Tippi walked her hands up her thighs and breathed hard; beads of perspiration mustachioed her upper lip. "I read where sitting makes our brains shrivel up and the cells explode and you have to live the rest of your life playing bingo and eating nothing but oatmeal and strained peas." She looked over Gert's shoulder and checked out her hand.

"I like bingo," Gert said.

Tippi tapped a flower tile on Gert's rack. "Don't say I didn't warn you," she called over her shoulder as she strode off.

The Goose Down Senior Citizens Center was bustling. Membership was on the rise; construction of the new media room and outside walking trails was complete and today, besides the games that were underway, the schedule included crafts, line dancing, and kazoo band practice. Tomorrow's big mahjong tournament heralded the official launch of the center's rebirth nearly a year after the shocking discovery that a popular center member had been found strangled in her lover's hot tub. The town and the senior center were beginning to heal and so were the relationships damaged in the hunt for a killer.

Tippi checked the pink band on her wrist and marched down the hall to the card room where Hank Klaber and his buddies were engaged in a game of Texas Hold'em.

"I'm putting lunch out. If you characters expect to eat, don't dilly-dally."

Hank, his eyes locked on his cards, gave her a thumb's up.

…

Tippi found an opened bag of coffee and used it to set up the large coffee urn. She was on the volunteer committee and made sure coffee was always available for the unending stream of members who filed through the center every day. Today as usual, a tray of pastries accompanied the coffee.

"Need some help?" Gert asked. She went to the sink and washed her hands before she slipped on plastic gloves and a hairnet. "I was dead on the next hand."

"Have a brownie." Tippi held out a plate of chocolate squares stacked in a pyramid. She popped one into her own mouth and filled a Styrofoam cup with coffee. "I better try one of these, too." She chose a lemon bar from a tray.

"No, thanks." Gert shuddered. "I can't even look at food. I'm bringing more of those in tomorrow for the tournament. I have so many leftovers from Ernie's wake, my big chest freezer in the basement is full." She wiped away a tear.

Tippi hugged her friend. "None of us can believe it, Gert. Your wedding finally gave us a reason to celebrate and then..." She licked powered sugar from her fingers.

"Everything happened so fast, I still can't believe he's gone. He just finished cutting hay out back and was all set to bale the following week when he got sick. I wanted to call the doctor but he got furious and wouldn't hear of it. He said it was just the flu and I should quit making a big deal out of it."

"Men are so stubborn."

Gert reached for a stack of paper plates. She started to move them to the serving table when they slipped out of her hands and scattered around her feet. She threw up her hands. "Now look what I've done. I'm jittery, I have a headache I can't shake, my stomach's upset. I'm a mess."

"Gert, It's only been two weeks. I remember when I lost L.T. I couldn't keep anything down. What finally turned me around was the half-gallon of black raspberry chocolate chip ice cream someone left in my freezer. I can thank Graeter's and the angel that left it for being the woman I am today."

That made Gert smile.

Tippi led her friend to a seat at the table while she cleaned up the plates and finished setting out the food. "I'm glad I could talk you in to coming back to the center."

Gert blew her nose in the napkin Tippi offered her. "The ER doctor said you'd be surprised at how many elderly people die of flu."

"Elderly? Pshaw, Ernie was only seventy-one. I'd hardly call that elderly."

Gert brushed tears from her cheeks. "Anyway, I'm glad to be back. I'm looking forward to beating you in the tournament tomorrow."

Tippi patted her friend's shoulder. "So, you're ready to throw down the gauntlet? Ordinarily, I'd take you up on that but this once—and don't expect me to admit this to anyone else ever—I hope you pull it off." Tippi turned her attention to setting up the rest of the lunch.

"Looks good. Should I call in the troops?"

Tippi nodded. "Okay but first..." She pointed her spatula to the desserts. "Pick your poison?"

"What the heck," Gert said, "might as well die with a smile on my face."

TWO

Big Roy Gates leaned back in his chair and rested his head against the garage door. He slid the plastic hose over his head and out of his nose and coiled it around the oxygen tank next to him. He shut off the tank, pulled a pack of cigarettes from his pocket, and lit up.

The warm sun had made him sleepy. He closed his eyes, the cigarette dangled from his fingers.

"I'll take one of those." Little Roy Gates ambled over and pulled up a seat. He wiggled the sausages he called fingers under his father's nose.

The senior Gates opened one eye before he handed over the pack. "I can tell you a place that sells them. You could buy 'em with some of those bad checks you were passing. I don't have the deep pockets your previous landlord has."

"Least in jail I didn't have to listen to you and Mom yapping at each other all day. And, thanks to the state of Ohio, I'm rehabilitated. Got my GED meaning I'm a official high school graduate. Whadda ya say about that, old man?"

"I say forty-six years old is a little late for getting out of high school."

Little Roy stubbed out his cigarette under the heel of his boot. He pulled a plug of chewing tobacco from his overall pocket and tucked it inside his cheek.

"You look like a damn squirrel," his father growled. He lit another cigarette with the one he was just finishing.

"Speaking of squirrels, you think the widow Schwab will let me hunt on her place now that the old man is gone? Lotsa squirrels and possums over there. I've seen a bunch of wild turkeys too."

His father had a coughing fit that brought a glob of spit to his lips. He wiped his mouth with the oversized white handkerchief he took from the chest pocket of his denim overalls.

Little Roy waited for his father to catch his breath. "One time when I was huntin' there, I ran into Ernie. He told me he put food out for the critters to keep them comin' onto the property. Went on and on about how he liked watching 'em and something 'bout protectin' them in a place called Perpatooty. You think that's in Ohio?"

"I think you're an idiot."

"Then he told me to beat it and posted a bunch of 'No Trespassing' signs."

The elder Roy took a long drag on his cigarette. "I say take your rifle and if the old lady or them damn Mexicans over there give you any trouble, shoot them."

Little Roy laughed so hard, he almost choked on his plug of tobacco. He spat a brown wad onto the driveway and wiped dribble off his chin with the back of his hand.

"You're a damn uncouth hillbilly." Big Roy scowled at his eldest namesake.

"I think I'll get my bro' to give me a hand puttin' my deer stand back up in her hickory-grove. I nailed me the biggest buck in the township back there last year. Remember, Pop?"

"I remember that's what you said." Big Roy pointed his chin towards their neighbor's property. "You should ride over there to take a look around. I'm guessing our widow lady's going to be out the rest of the day because of the goings-on over at the senior center. I'm on my way there myself to play a little Texas Hold'em. I intend to knock that smartass Hank Klaber down a peg or two."

"I'll kick Baby outta his rack and fire up the ATV after I git me somethin' to eat. You need anything from the house?"

"Bring me a two-liter Mountain Dew and that bag of pork rinds I hid in the gun safe so your ma can't get to them. The woman has no respect for personal property." He jiggled the oxygen tank and held it out. "I need a new tank of air too. I think this one's empty."

Little Roy grunted as he tried to hoist his over-size body from the metal folding chair. Already, the chair seat was concave and the legs were beginning to buckle.

"Damn it, Little Roy. You go through them chairs faster than an old woman goes through the line at a free cheese giveaway at the senior center. "

Little Roy wiggled loose and got to his feet. He farted twice and waddled inside.

...

Big Roy wheezed as he dragged his tank of oxygen behind him on the way to his truck. Gracella, GG for short, Roy and Velma's middle child, slid into the passenger seat and set Big Roy's tank on the floor between her legs.

"Here's your lunch, Pa." Little Roy handed a plastic sack with the soda and the coveted pork rinds to his sister.

"Say 'hey' to all your fellow garbage collectors at the hospital, sis."

GG gave him the finger. "Least I got a job. And we're housekeeping, moron, not garbage collectors." She grunted as she worked to stretch the seatbelt around her belly.

Baby Roy, number three child and last of the 'Roy' trio, draped his arms over the passenger's side window. "Give those geezers what for, Pa," he said. He snapped open his Bic and pointed the flame at the cigarette clinging to his lip.

His father reached out and smacked the lighter out of his son's hand. "You trying to blow us to kingdom come? This tank isn't full of candy, dumbass."

"Sorry, Pa." Baby Roy hung his head and stared at the ground. The last of the Gates' brood, Baby was the spitting image of his father; tall and wiry, eyes set close together, his hair stringy and beginning to thin. But, that's where the likeness ended, for Big had a reputation as being smart, some said shrewd, others said sly. At first glance, the old man might be easy to underestimate if one didn't know that upon graduation from high school, he'd been offered a baseball scholarship to the University of Cincinnati where he planned to major in business. That game was called when Velma threw him a curve ball—she was pregnant. In short order, the Gates' were reduced to a farm team and Baby's arrival heralded strike three.

Big Roy revved the engine and shouted at his sons, "Now, get out of my way, losers." The truck wheels spit dirt and gravel in their wake as he sped down the drive.

. . .

Baby clung to his brother as Little Roy steered the ATV through the weeds and honeysuckle that separated the Gates' farm from Gert and Ernie Schwab's. The motor whined under their weight as they bumped along hillocks and swerved around piles of cow dung. They drove past a group of Black Angus cattle that paused grazing only briefly as the brothers drove by.

The gate to the bottom fields and the stocked pond was open when the men crested the hill. Baby leaned over his brother's shoulder and pointed to a black truck parked beside the bank of Paddy's Run creek. Little Roy hit the gas and followed a cow path down the hill, coming to a stop next to the pickup. The brothers watched as two men in waders waved as they climbed out of the stream and started towards them.

"Howdy," the taller of the two men greeted the Gates'. The men carried cameras and sported lime-green windbreakers with a logo of a tree and the initials CLAW emblazoned across the front.

Little Roy sneered at the men. "Hey." He lifted his rifle from the seat beside him and handed it to Baby.

"You fellas live around here?" the second man asked.

"Yep," Little Roy answered. "Next door. We's the Gates." He shook off Baby and hoisted his trunk-like legs over the seat. Once he got out of the vehicle and got his balance, he turned to face the two strangers. "What's CLAW?"

"Get right to the point, do you? I like that. I'm Stephen and this here is Harvey." Stephen offered Little Roy his hand. "I didn't see you guys at the meeting last night. I think it might have been your daddy I spoke to? Roy Gates?"

"That'd be Big Roy. I'm Little Roy and this here's my brother, Baby Roy."

"Like the Georges, huh?" Harvey said with a smile.

"Who?" Baby asked.

"You know, the Foreman's? George...?" Harvey started to say.

"Yeah, whatever," Little Roy sniggered. He turned back to Stephen who had put his hand in his pocket. "What the hell is CLAW and what are you doing on Schwab's property?"

Baby rested the butt of the rifle on his thigh.

Harvey brought out his cell phone and placed his thumb on the nine so the men could see it.

"Who you gonna call? That moron Sheriff Grange?" Little Roy sneered.

Baby let out a high-pitched cackle from where he was sitting on the quad. "That's rich." He pointed a bony finger at Harvey. "You think he cares what happens to two skinny white boys name a' CLAW who's obviously trespassing? Youse are dumbasses," he added.

"Now, fellas." Stephen looked nervously from Little Roy to Baby who fingered the trigger on his gun. He held up one hand and reached into his jacket pocket with the other. "Let me give you one of these brochures about what's going on around here. Like I said, we had a meeting..."

All four men jumped at the sound of another vehicle approaching the top of the hill. A helmeted figure in a yellow jumpsuit crouched over the handlebars of a large black Harley. A black helmet, topped with a bright red cockscomb, was all that showed over the hood of the bike's sidecar. The driver paused, then gunned the engine and sped toward the spot where the group stood.

The men scattered as cyclist and passenger bounced over the uneven earth before coming to a halt inches from the truck.

Red curls cascaded to the driver's shoulders as she shook off the helmet. Blue eyes crinkled at the shocked faces of the men who reassembled around the bike. "Hey Steve, Harvey," Carin Seitz greeted the men from CLAW before turning her attention to Little Roy and Baby. "And, what are you two misfits doing on my daddy's property? Did ya' get lost again?"

THREE

Tippi smiled as the man in her life, Hank Klaber, pushed a cartload of folding chairs down the hall. They'd met three years ago on a trip with the senior center to Euro Disney and had been together ever since. Hank, who kept his pockets full of the chocolates she loved or was sitting center front when she performed her comedy routine at Gaggle of Giggles, had come into Tippi's life as a wonderful surprise. After losing Teddy his freshman year at Dartmouth when cancer took her and L.T's only child, then came back for her husband of forty-three years, she'd thanked God for what she'd had and made peace with the idea of living out her days on her own. But here she was, in love again, although she had only recently admitted it to herself and certainly hadn't informed Hank. That was a step Tippi was still afraid to take.

Someday I'll tell him. Right now, I've got a tournament to run. Her stomach rumbled and soft lights swirled before her eyes. She stopped and put her hand on the wall to steady herself. *Pull yourself together, woman. You need more coffee.* She stiffened her shoulders and hurried down the hall.

...

Hank finished setting up two card tables in the lounge for the men who'd accompanied their wives to the mahjong tournament. He was about to close the sliding door that separated the area from the noisy room where the games were already underway with the sounds of clicking game tiles, women calling out plays and boisterous laughter peppering the air.

He spotted Gert watching from the sidelines. "Can you keep the ladies in check, Gert? Big money at stake on this side."

Gert turned the palms of her hands up in a gesture of helplessness as Hank waved and slid the door shut.

Gert surveyed the room before she wound her way through the tables to a corner where Violet Schmidt was playing. "I'm not feeling too well," she whispered in Violet's ear. "I'm going to lie down in the clinic. Would you mind helping with lunch in my place?" she asked.

Violet looked up from her tiles. "Don't worry, I'll take care of it. We're done here." She took Gert's hand and looked closer at her friend. "You look terrible. Maybe we should get someone to drive you home."

"No." Gert forced a smile. "I just need to close my eyes for a few minutes. I'll be fine."

...

Tippi leaned against the kitchen counter with a brownie in one hand and her cellphone in the other. A sprinkle of chocolate crumbs decorated her chest. She shook the phone a few times and glared at the screen "I think this thing is broken," she told Violet.

"What's the matter?"

She set the brownie on the counter and twisted the pink band on her wrist. "This stupid bracelet is supposed to record every step I take and show it on my phone and it's not working. I'm supposed to walk ten thousand steps every day and it says I'm only up to three hundred fifty-six. If I make my goal, I can eat anything I want and still lose weight." She pumped her arm a few times and re-checked her phone. "There, now I'm at four hundred."

"That's cheating."

"Is not," Tippi swung her arms.

"Let me know how this latest *diet* works for you."

Arcella Alvarez smiled at the women while she busied herself lining up the pans of food. Her husband, Victor set out the freshly filled coffee urns.

Tippi wiped chocolate from her mouth and took a tube of lipstick from her pocket. She squinted into the window on the microwave and slathered on a fresh coat of color. *"Pretty in Pink."* She smacked her lips and held the tube out to show Arcella.

"Nice," Arcella agreed. She inclined her head toward the steaming trays of food. "Lunch gonna get cold."

"Right-o. I'm on it."

The players had cleared the game tiles and cards from the tables and were waiting for the signal that lunch was ready when Tippi marched in to the center of the room. She was a commanding presence in a pink velour tracksuit set off by pink and white tennis shoes. With the recently added pink swath through her halo of white curls, Tippi resembled a six-foot high strawberry cupcake topped with pink and vanilla frosting.

"Game over," she shouted above the fracas.

The volume in the room escalated as players groaned and cheered. Tippi reached a hand into the neck of her jacket and retrieved a silver whistle. She blew one ear-shattering blast.

Her voice boomed, "Be sure to put your points on the whiteboard by the door. Bathroom down the hall to the left. Lunch in five. Entertainment right after. Play resumes in forty-five."

The players laughed, pushed, and elbowed their way into the lunch line while they rehashed the morning's games. The Alvarezes refilled the serving dishes while Tippi and Violet assisted in between bites from their own generous helpings. Hank brought up the end of the line behind the men and watched the platefuls of food disappear.

"I can't believe this is all that's left." Hank sighed as he looked down at his plate of wilted salad. "Not even a cookie." He eyed the empty trays and scored a few telltale crumbs.

"You should have planned ahead like I did." Tippi leaned across the counter and took a bite out of her bread. She marched in place a few steps and checked her phone.

"You could share."

"I could but now that I'm on this exercise program, I have to keep up my strength. I was feeling weak." She shielded her plate with her hand.

Hank stalked off with his salad and a bottle of water. When he was out of striking distance, he called over his shoulder, "Hey, Tabitha, those pants make your ass look bigger than Kim Kardashian's."

He pulled up a seat beside the other poker players. He eyed Big Roy Gates' bag of pork rinds and two-liter bottle of Mountain Dew. "Your lunch looks better than mine. Care to share?"

Big Roy answered by shaking the crumbs from the bag directly into his mouth.

"Hurry up, Hank," Bob Applebee said, as he rolled his wheelchair up to the table where the men sat. "The band is waiting."

Hank rolled his eyes. "This day just gets better and better. Let's get it over with."

"I'll share my apple with you afterward," Applebee said. "That is, if you stop whining."

Hank joined the other members of The Honkers, the center's kazoo band, at the front of the room. The band members, except for Hank, sported white, collared shirts with pockets emblazoned with a Canada goose rising above the words, *Goose Down Honkers*, embroidered in black. On the back, an almost life-size replica of the bird soared above each kazooist's name. Hank told Applebee there was no way he'd wear that getup hoping it would disqualify him from membership. Instead, Applebee told him he could wear a plain, white polo which would mean he was assistant band director and as such, responsible for making sure the instruments were kept in working order and Violet always had plenty of catgut on hand for her washtub-cello.

Applebee locked his leg braces at the knees and allowed Victor to help him to stand so he could conduct from the podium. The band opened with the new song they'd been practicing, *Won't You Come Home, Bill Bailey,* followed by their usual repertoire.

"Everybody on your feet for *The Chicken Dance*," Applebee commanded. "Let's give those new joints Medicare bought you a real workout."

The band blew their kazoos, Violet played the washtub with gusto and after two 'encores', the Hooters gave up and filed back to their game tables.

"That was one of our best performances yet," Violet wheezed as she walked with Tippi back to her table. When she caught her breath, she wiped perspiration from her forehead and said, "Will you take my place in the next game? I want to check on Gert."

"I'll try, but my stomach is a little queasy so I can't promise how well I'll do."

"Just how many desserts did you have?" Violet laughed.

Tippi pulled out a chair and nodded to the three women seated around the table. She sat down and smiled up at her friend. "I was only trying to keep up with you, Vi."

***

Violet opened the door to the empty clinic and set two cups of coffee on top of the new file cabinet. She sipped from one of the cups as she thought back to the night a killer held Tippi and six year-old Marcy captive in this very room. She could picture Hank risking his own life getting the two to safety and then protecting the rest of them by offering himself as a hostage. It struck her how suddenly something could trigger a rush of memories of that terrible time almost a year later.

She finished her drink and crumpled the empty cup before tossing it in the trash. A wave of nausea washed over but she brushed it off. *Shouldn't have had that third brownie.* She took a long drink from the second cup of coffee to ease the stomach cramps that were beginning to grow more intense. She stepped into the hallway, almost upsetting Arcella carrying an armload of items Gert had brought from home for the occasion.

"Have you seen Gert?" Violet asked.

"No, Miss. Is something wrong?"

"She said she wasn't feeling well and went to lie down but I just came from the clinic and she isn't there." Violet patted Arcella on the shoulder. "I'm sure she's fine. You go ahead, I'll find her."

Violet went into the women's restroom and knocked on the stall door. "Gert, is that you? Everything alright?"

There was no answer. She knocked harder and bent down to look under the door. She could see a pair of black pumps but there was still no answer.

"Gert, I'm going to look under the door unless you answer me and tell me you're okay. Gert?"

Violet lay down on her stomach and was about to put her head under the door when Tippi rushed into the room. She held her hands over her mouth and gagged as she ran into the end stall.

"Tippi? What's going on?" Violet struggled to her feet.

Retching noises came from Tippi's stall at the end of the row.

"Hold on, I'm going for help. I'll be right back."

Violet hurried down the hall. Instead of laughing and the clicking of mahjong tiles, she heard hacking coughs and moans coming from the tournament room. She froze. It looked like a scene from a Hollywood disaster movie: everywhere, people groaned and clutched their stomachs while others lay still where they had fallen, their lips blue and slick with a bloody substance that pooled against chalky skin. Victor attempted to assist stricken players while others clustered in corners, horrified.

Hank appeared at Violet's side. "I called 911." His eyes searched the room for those familiar pink and white curls. He'd almost lost Tippi once and he wasn't about to let anything happen to her now. "Have you seen...?"

"Bathroom," Violet gasped. She clasped her hand to her mouth and collapsed at Hank's feet.

Sirens from Goose Down's nearby law enforcement and fire departments wailed in the background.

A cruiser sped up the long hill to the center, siren blaring. The officer swerved to avoid a beat-up pickup truck as it sped away from the scene. "What the hell?"

Hank was waiting outside as the patrol car screeched to a halt. "Hurry up, Pete. Down the hall."

Sheriff Peter Grange surveyed the room and drew a ragged breath.

FOUR

"Good afternoon, Carin. How are you this fine day?" Stephen welcomed her with a warm smile. "I saw your hubby at the meeting last night and mentioned we had scheduled an appointment with your dad to walk the property today. Gert gave me the okay to go ahead but I don't think Norm was too pleased."

"That must have been one heck of a meeting you all had. I didn't go to bed until after Colbert and Norman still wasn't home."

"It got pretty heated," Harvey said with a sidelong glance at Stephen.

Carin walked around the bike to the sidecar where the helmet bobbed restlessly. "What do you want?" She said, as she removed her passenger's headgear.

"Woof."

"Okay, Sauerkraut. Out."

The German Shepard jumped up and took his place beside his owner. His muscular haunches quivered as he eyed the men.

"Sit," Carin directed. The animal complied but remained alert as he surveyed the group.

"What kind of stupid name is Sauerkraut?" Baby Roy

snickered.

Sauerkraut turned his gaze on the man and snarled.

"He doesn't appreciate anybody disrespecting him," Sauerkraut's owner said.

"Anyway," Stephen interjected, "we're all done here, Carin. We'll be getting our report written up and CLAW will be in touch with Gert. Probably take a few months as we're getting a lot of inquiries from folks wanting to talk with us."

"I'm asking again, buddy. What the hell is CLAW?" Little Roy took a menacing step toward Stephen and Harvey.

Sauerkraut growled and stood up. The hairs on his back rose.

Baby cocked his gun.

"Let's all settle down," Stephen said.

Harvey handed brochures to the Gates men. "Conserving Land And Waterways."

"Huh?" Baby scanned the brochure Harvey gave him and crumpled it up and tossed it on the ground.

Harvey stooped to retrieve the paper. "CLAW. It stands for 'Conserving Land And Waterways'. We're a nonprofit group working with the Ohio EPA to protect the Great Miami aquifer. We're talking with local farmers about putting conservation easements on their property. Your daddy was real interested and…"

"What language is he speaking?" Little Roy asked Baby.

"I think it's Chinese or Mex-ee-can-eee," Baby chimed in. The brothers thought that was hilarious.

"I think it's time you boys went home," Carin told the Gates. "Me and these men have some business to discuss and you all are getting on Sauerkraut's nerves. I can't be responsible if you continue to tick him off."

Sauerkraut, hearing his name, took a step toward Baby.

"Let's get outta here, Baby," Little Roy said. "We'll come back when it ain't so crowded."

"If you fellas could read," Carin said, "you'd know that those signs say 'No Trespassing'. That means..."

"I know what it means. You better watch your tongue or..."

Little Roy was stopped from finishing his thought when Carin's cell phone beeped. She walked away from the group to take the call and returned a few seconds later, pale and shaking. "I have to go," she said, addressing Stephen and Harvey. "Something happened at the senior center."

She faced the Gates' who had climbed back into their vehicle. "Get out of here." She let go of Sauerkraut's collar. The dog stood poised, waiting for her command.

Little Roy turned on the ignition and started off. As they reached the crest of the hill, Baby fired a parting shot into the air.

...

A sheriff's deputy waved Carin to a stop when she pulled up to the entrance of the center where ambulances, a fire-truck and several sheriff's vehicles sat, their lights flashing, sirens hushed in deadly silence.

"Officer, what happened?" Carin got off the bike. She scanned the scene in front of her.

The deputy ignored her question. "The center is closed. You need to move your vehicle."

"I received a call from Hank Klaber to come right over. My, uh," she hesitated, "my stepmother is Gert Schwab. She's taken ill."

"Hang on." The deputy turned away and spoke into his radio. Carin strained to hear but only caught the end. "Oh, Jesus."

"What?" Carin became increasingly agitated. "I need to go in. Gert..." She stopped when she saw Hank hurrying toward her. "Hank? Is Gert okay?"

Hank put his long arm around her waist and nodded at the deputy who looked stricken. He took Carin's keys and tossed them to the officer. "Let's go in. Come on Sauerkraut."

Inside, Carin and Hank stepped aside as two stretchers moved past them. Visitors and senior center members mixed with law enforcement officers, paramedics and firefighters. EMTs attempted to triage the sickest of the victims as emergency crews helped those still standing into the lounge.

Hank guided Carin and Sauerkraut into an empty room and closed the door. They could hear the muffled sounds of this latest disaster around them.

"Hank, you're scaring me. Is Gert okay? Tell me."

Hank rubbed his eyes and coughed before he spoke. His voice cracked, "No, Carin. She's not."

Carin gasped and covered her mouth with both hands.

"I'm so sorry, honey." He wrapped his arms around her. "We don't know what happened for sure but Gert was gone before the paramedics even got here."

"I can't believe it. This is all some horrible nightmare."

"I know, sweetie."

"First Dad, now this." Carin broke down and wept.

Hank offered her a napkin from his pocket.

Carin blew her nose. "What do I do now? Do I call somebody? Dad and I are—were—the only family she had." Shaken, Carin looked to Hank.

"I'll find out more for you from Sheriff Grange," Hank said. They watched as another stretcher carrying a person wrapped in a blanket was rushed down the hallway to a waiting ambulance.

"I'll call Norm and tell him what's happened," Hank said. He searched his pockets for his cellphone. He retrieved a crumpled Hershey bar wrapper, three foil-covered candies and a pink ribbon but no phone.

A slight smile brushed Carin's lips.

"Tippi," he said by way of an explanation. "I must have left the darn phone in the car again."

A young deputy poked her head into the room. "Hank?"

"Hey, Moira. What's up?"

"I thought you should know," Deputy Moira Potts paused and looked at Carin, "Tippi…"

Hank leaped to his feet. "Tippi? What about Tippi?"

"She's sick, Hank. They're taking her to Memorial. She's asking for you." Moira blinked hard. "I think you better go with her."

Hank looked frantically at another stretcher being shuttled toward the door. Two paramedics working over the victim blocked his view.

"I'll stay with Carin." Moira stepped in.

Carin squeezed Hank's hand. "It's okay. You go. I'll pray for Tippi."

...

Hank threaded his way through the crowded Emergency

Department waiting room to the desk marked 'Registration'. He jammed his fists into his pockets. When it was finally his turn at the window, a harried-looking young woman scrolled down her computer screen before she glanced up at him.

"I'm with Tabitha Mulgrew." Hank winced. Tippi hated the name.

"How are you related?"

"Fiancé," Hank replied without hesitation.

The registrar turned back to her computer. "I'll let the doctor know you're here. Please have a seat..."

"I need to see her now."

"I'm sorry, sir. You'll have to wait until someone can talk to you. If you'd rather, you can give me your cell phone number and I'll call you when you can go back. You might be more comfortable in the family lounge." She pointed to a room next to the chapel, "or, in the cafeteria." She locked eyes with Hank. "It could be a while."

Hank reacted as he often did when he felt life spiraling out of control. "Don't tell me I have to wait. I need to see her *now*—not when you get around to it." He regretted the words the minute he spoke.

"I know this is hard, sir."

"I'm sorry. It's just..." Hank retrieved his cell phone from his pocket and looked up the number. The phone was new and he'd only gotten it at Tippi's insistence after last year's crisis at the center. He jotted down his name and number on the back of a crumpled Costco receipt he found in his pocket and slid it across the desk. "Thank you. Do you have friends...?" He tilted his head at the crowded room.

"My aunt," she said and wiped a tear. "She was at the mahjong tournament today. She'd been looking forward to it for weeks."

"What's her name?"

"Violet. Violet Schmidt."

"Oh, no. Violet and I are in the band together. I was with her when she collapsed. Is she okay?"

"I don't know. I'm waiting to hear too."

Hank reached out and squeezed her hand. "Let's stay positive, okay?"

She nodded wearily and looked around Hank at the people behind him.

Hank realized he was holding up the line. "I'll let you get back to work. And, I'm sorry I was such an ass."

FIVE

Sheriff Grange busied himself setting up a command post in the nurse's office at the center. He'd instructed his deputies to interview everyone present who either had not become ill or who refused efforts to take them to the ED. When they finished here, he'd have them follow up on the victims who had been taken away by ambulance. Memorial was a small community hospital not equipped to handle large-scale emergencies, so some of the victims had been taken to University in Cincinnati.

He rubbed his temples and was about to make a call when Deputy Moira Potts poked her head inside the room.

"I didn't get to tell you before but I'm glad you're back, sir." Moira offered her boss a soft smile.

"If I'd known all hell was going to break loose, I'd have taken a couple more weeks off." The sheriff rubbed his knee. "Damn physical therapists are a bunch of sadists. Hurt worse than the surgery itself."

"So I've heard." The entire office had been subjected to Grange's tirades during his convalescence when he made his twice-daily calls to the office following his knee replacement surgery. Moira changed the subject. "Need anything, Sheriff?"

"I could use a pot of coffee, a couple of sandwiches and a slice of pie." He grinned at his new recruit.

"You must have a cast-iron stomach, Sir. I couldn't even look at food after seeing all this." Moira shuddered.

"Well, I been at this job for a while and not that we see much on this scale in Goose Down, I have learned to keep myself fueled up and ready."

Moira turned her head and covered her mouth to stifle a laugh. The sheriff was not known for skipping meals, a fact reflected in his expanding waistline.

"All that other stuff I said is because I was running late this morning," he paused, a deep red blush crept up his neck, "and I missed breakfast." He didn't have to mention that the reason he was late this morning and every morning since he'd returned to work, was because his new lady friend, Amy Spencer, was spending all her evenings, mornings and any free time in-between, with the Sheriff. Their romance was the talk of Goose Down.

"Do you want me to make a pot of coffee?"

"Well, now, seeing as how we don't know the cause of all these folks taking sick and that one person has died—so far—whatever remains of their lunch is evidence. I think it best, deputy, if we send out for the coffee."

"I'm sorry, Sheriff. I meant..." She gave up and looked down at her feet.

"It's alright. You can't learn it all overnight. This isn't exactly typical for Goose Down, now is it?"

"No, sir. It sure isn't." Moira brightened and said, "How about if I ask a couple of the men we already interviewed to run over to the diner? I imagine these crews are going to be here awhile and could use some refreshment."

"Excellent thinking, Deputy. Get right on it. And," he added, "don't forget the pie." He leaned back in his chair, clasped his hands behind his head. "Chocolate cream is my favorite."

Grange's cell phone rang. "It's the hospital."

Moira waited.

The Sheriff held the phone to his ear. "You go ahead, Deputy. I got this."

Grange waited until Moira left and pushed the door shut behind her. "Grange." He leaned over the desk and cradled his head in his free hand as he listened to the voice on the phone. "Thanks for letting me know. You'll keep me apprised?"

He ended the call and walked to the window. It was the window Tippi and Marcy had used in their escape from a madman last year as the trail leading to a killer grew warmer. Grange never imagined that such evil would ever come to his town, but it had. And now the call from the hospital informed him Violet and Tippi were in critical condition and their prognoses were poor.

Grange replayed Ernie's death over in his mind. He tried to wrap his head around the idea of attending another funeral. *I pray to God this doesn't get any worse. I don't know how much more this town can take.*

. . .

Norman Seitz swung his silver Hummer into the 'No Parking' spot behind the fire-truck at the senior center. He placed the placard reading 'Official Business: Township Trustee' on the dashboard and pulled a cold Dr. Pepper from the vehicle's refrigerated console. He smiled into the mirror above the visor, wet one finger with his tongue and smoothed his eyebrows before he stepped out into the warm air of the late afternoon.

Deputy Moira Potts watched him from her post and stuck the remains of her turkey sandwich into her pocket when she greeted him at the front door. "Evening, sir." She made a notation of Norm's name, arrival time and purpose of his visit in her iPad. "I'll need you to sign here, sir." She wiped some telltale mayonnaise on her pant leg and pointed to where he should sign with a glittery pink nail. "Carin is waiting for you."

Norman scribbled down his signature and flashed a dazzling mouthful of teeth.

Moira frowned and looked over his shoulder. "That's a beautiful car, sir.

"Thank you, Moira," he said reading the nameplate on her pocket. "Maybe someday I'll take you for a spin," he flirted.

Moira squared her shoulders and looked him in the eyes. "Yes, sir. But now I'll have to ask you to move it. That area is reserved for the emergency vehicles."

"It's fine. I'm with the county, Deputy." Norm brushed a loose strand of blonde hair from his eyes. "I know I can count on you to keep an eye on her, right, sweetheart?" He lifted Moira's hand to his lips and went inside.

"Jerk," Moira said under her breath. She debated on whether or not to give him a ticket for parking in a fire lane and settled for squeezing the remainder of the mayonnaise packet from her lunch on the inside of the driver's door handle. She smeared it around and stood back to admire her handiwork. *Take that, sweetheart.*

. . .

Bob Applebee waved across the foyer. "Over here, Norm."

The younger man folded his lean, six foot four frame into a squat so he was face-to-face with Applebee. He took a long drink of his soda before he spoke again. "What the hell is going on?"

"It's a mess in there. The morning went fine. Big mahjong tournament, Texas Hold'em, then lunch, the band performed and..."

Norman cracked a thin smile. "They couldn't face the music?"

Applebee frowned. "Nobody's laughing, Norm."

"Bad joke. I'm sorry."

"I'm betting on food poisoning. It was about an hour or more after that everybody started getting sick."

"Everyone?" Norm blanched.

"Everyone who ate lunch."

"My God, Bob, what the hell did they serve?"

"Lasagna and..."

"And Gert?" Norm interrupted. Sweat beaded on his forehead.

"We learned she wasn't feeling well when she came in this morning."

Norman stood up and shook out one leg, then the other. He smoothed the creases on his jeans and re-tucked his silk shirt, his hand drifting to the Roberto Cavalli label on the waistband. "This is going to be tough on Carin. First her dad, now, Gert. Not only that but we're going to have to figure out what to do with the farm."

"Maybe Victor and ..."

"Right, the Mexicans."

"Guatemalans."

"Say what?"

"They're from Guatemala."

"Whatever," Norman said. "I told Schwab not to get mixed up with that outfit. No telling what kind of people they are. I don't trust 'um."

"They came highly recommended to the pastor at St. Mathias. Victor has a degree in agriculture and worked as a manager on a coffee plantation in San Benito. He and Arcella fled when a drug cartel swept in and massacred more than twenty farm workers—including children. Victor and Arcella barely made it out alive. You and Carin are lucky to have them looking after the place."

An officer opened the door. "Carin's here."

Norman shook Applebee's hand. "I'll see you later." He started to walk away then turned back to Applebee. "I want to call you later to get your thoughts on the meeting last night. Those guys from CLAW sure got everybody riled up. Wonder what your take on that whole deal is?"

Applebee nodded. "Right now, CLAW is the least of my worries." He waved over his shoulder as he wheeled away. "Adios, amigo."

SIX

"What are you doin' home already?" Velma looked up at her husband from a half-finished jigsaw puzzle. "Was them boys mean to you?" She turned back to the puzzle and fit a piece into the border. The picture on the box showed a red barn in a snowstorm and an old horse standing beside a split-rail fence. "Remind me not to buy any more puzzles of snow. I been working on this damn thing for a month."

Big Roy reached into the fridge and helped himself to a Mountain Dew. "Nobody was mean to me, old woman. I'm home because a bunch of those geezers got sick. It was disgusting." He took a long swig of his drink. "I hightailed it outta there as fast as I could. Just in the nick of time too—I passed the sheriff in the driveway. Would have been stuck there for a month of Sundays while that old fool tried to figure out what was as plain as the nose on your face."

"Yeah? What's that?"

"Gluttony, pure and simple. They were pushing and shoving their way into that lunch line like they hadn't eaten in a month." He drained his soda. "Grab me another cold one while you're up, will

33

you, Vel?" He waved the empty can at his wife.

"I ain't up." Velma huffed and hefted herself out of her chair. She shuffled across the room and grabbed a 2-liter that she slammed on the table in front of her husband. She filled a glass with ice and slid it across the table.

"You know what Reverend Meister says about gluttony," Velma said, as if her husband should know.

"No, I can't say I do."

"You would if you'd come with me to…"

"Don't start on me, old woman. That old fraud is only after one thing and that's lining his pockets with my money. The last time I was in church was on our wedding day forty-three years ago and I'll be in a pine box the next time so stop singing that old tune."

"Anyway," Velma said, "gluttony is a deadly sin. It says so right in the Bible." She looked smug. "They will reap what they sow. The Rev says that too."

Big Roy picked up his car key and used it to clean the dirt from under his fingernails.

"Talk about disgusting," Velma said.

"When you get a job and start payin' the bills around here, you can have a say about what I can and what I cannot do. Until then, keep your opinions to yourself."

"I don't call collecting social security exactly a job."

"It's called reaping what I sowed, woman. You and Mister Meister know all about that.

Velma couldn't think of a retort so she turned her attention back to her puzzle.

Roy flipped on the battered, portable television he kept on the kitchen table. He adjusted the old set's rabbit ears until he could make out the shadowy figure of a woman standing in front of a low building. He lit up a cigar and turned up the sound.

The reporter spoke from the edge of a parking lot crowded with emergency vehicles and uniformed men and women hustling in and out of the building behind her. "Law enforcement and paramedics are at the scene of an unfolding situation here at the Goose Down Senior Citizens' Center. The center was hosting a large mahjong tournament today when participants became violently ill following lunch." She put a hand to her earphone and listened before she continued the broadcast. "We have just been informed that one person, Gert Schwab, has died and several others have been taken to local hospitals. At this time, we do not know their conditions. You may recall this was the scene of a murder last year. Now, it looks as though another disaster has struck. We will keep you updated on this breaking news story as information becomes available."

Velma looked over at the screen. "Gert's dead?" She looked to her husband for confirmation

Roy flipped off the television. "That's what she said."

"I can't believe it, Big. I just got a note from her yesterday thanking me for the stuff I took for Ernie's wake. That Mexican woman…

"Guatemalan," Big said.

"Whatever. The *Guatemalan* woman brought my plate back with a thank you note from Gert." She rummaged in the pocket of her housecoat and brought out a crumpled tissue. She blew her nose and wiped away a tear then, slipping a puzzle piece into place, said, "They better not cancel bingo tomorrow."

. . .

CLAW's offices, located in the Fernald Preserve, were dark. The hour was late so the parking lot the agency shared with the visitors' center was empty except for cars belonging to Stephen Ober and Harvey Johnson.

The men were returning to the office after a long day in the field. Stephen parked the company van next to his Jeep. He swung his legs out of the vehicle and slung his parka and briefcase over his arm. "I'm going to go for a walk before I start on this report," he told Harvey. "I need to clean the cobwebs out of my head."

"I hear you," Harvey said. He gathered up the camera bag, binoculars and surveying instruments vital to their work. "I can take your stuff in and get a pot of coffee started."

Stephen handed over his gear and started down one of the dimly lit walking trails that crisscrossed the sprawling parkland. He followed the wooden walkway and stopped to sit on the bench at one of the overlooks. As he watched a mother deer and her baby disappear into the brush, he marveled at the way nature had reclaimed the wetlands, marshes and grasslands from the silos and slag heaps of radioactive waste from the time Fernald was a nuclear weapons plant. He loved his job as Executive Director of CLAW and never once regretted his pledge to devote himself to protecting the natural beauty of this small corner of the world.

. . .

Stephen hung up his parka and went into the kitchen where Harvey finished making a fresh pot of coffee."

"Just what I need—caffeine." He rinsed out a mug with the agency logo emblazoned on it. "I've got that report on last night's meeting to finish and email to Columbus before I can go home."

"That meeting did a number on me," Harvey said as he opened a box of granola bars and helped himself before offering one to his colleague. "What I need you to explain to me..." He dunked the bar in his coffee and chewed before he went on, "Is why was that crowd so hostile?"

"I guess what we're offering sounds too good to be true. And the fact that the government is involved doesn't help. They're sure big brother is going to tell them what they can and can't do on their own land."

"But all we're saying is that a land trust on their property will protect them from those jackals itching to turn this county into one big development with strip malls and big box stores every ten feet..." He bit off another chunk of his bar.

"You're preaching to the choir, Harv."

"AND, they don't have to change the way they run their farms, AND, we're going to pay them to do it! Now how is any of that a bad thing? Tell me." He shook his head.

Stephen shrugged. "Our dollars can't compete with the big money the developers are promising. Our angle has to be reminding folks what Fernald did to the land, the water. We sure as hell don't want to go back there."

"That Norman Seitz is a piece of work. He's going to be trouble. He's been talking down the program all over the county." Harvey refilled his mug and offered the pot to Stephen.

"I don't know how his involvement is going to play out."

Stephen held out his cup. "Ernie's widow says she wants to go forward with the easement on their farm. Says it's what Ernie wanted."

"At least Bob Applebee provided a voice of reason. That's one township trustee on the planning board who's on our side."

Stephen nodded. "I better get to work. You sticking around?"

"No, I'm going to shut down my computer and call it a night."

Harvey went into his office and checked his email. He clicked on the Web icon for a last look at the day's headlines when a local news story caught his attention.

"What the...?" He scanned the page. "Hey, Stephen," he shouted, "Check this out. Gert Schwab is dead. They think it was food poisoning. At the senior center." He called out the details as he read through the brief account of what was known so far.

Stephen was headed toward Harvey's office when his phone rang. He let the call go to voicemail and listened.

"Is this CLAW?" a raspy voice wheezed. "Anybody there? Oh, hell."

Stephen heard the sound of a hacking cough before the voice spoke again. "Big Roy Gates here. We need to talk."

...

Zenobia Hachett cursed as she pulled the coroner's van into the lot at the senior center. "Damn that Norm. Idiot thinks he can put his little sign in the window and park any place he wants." She parked directly behind the Hummer and set the van's alarm.

"Hey, Moira," Zenobia's raspy voice called out to the young woman guarding the front door. "Hear you got quite a scene in there." She inclined her head toward the building.

Moira noted the coroner's arrival on her tablet. "Evening, Doctor." She held out the pad for her to sign. "The sheriff is expecting you."

"Thanks." Dr. Hachett propped her medical bag between her feet. Her bifocals dangled from a chain of colored glass beads and bounced across her chest as she dug through a red leather handbag. "Damn purse. Can never find anything—ah-ha, there you are." She held up a crumpled pack of cigarettes. "Wouldn't have a light on you, would you?"

Moira shook her head. "Sorry. Never smoked."

"Good for you. Nasty habit. Probably kill me one day." The doctor brought the cigarette pack to her nose and inhaled deeply. "That'll have to do." She sighed and dropped the pack into her bag. She tossed the fringed end of her wildly colorful pashmina over her shoulder. "You need anything, deputy? Bottle of water? Coffee?"

"No, thanks, I'm fine."

Dr. Hachett set her glasses on the end of her nose and looked at Moira over the top of the round black frames. "Be sure to ask for a break when you need it. These men don't think about stuff like that so we ladies need to stick together."

The older woman liked the young deputy and felt protective towards her. Years of working as the county coroner in what remained mostly a masculine domain had taught her to assert herself when she was on the job. She'd worked hard to establish herself as a competent and thorough investigator and had earned the respect of her peers as well as the voters who continued to elect her to the post year after year. Through years of fighting stereotypes as a medical student at the University of Cincinnati in the sixties, Zenobia had emerged as both strong and compassionate, qualities essential in her work.

A fireman came to the door and directed the doctor to the office where Grange waited for her. "Hi, Pete," she greeted the sheriff.

"Doc. How are you?" Sheriff Grange rubbed his eyes and looked up from the clutter spread out in front of him.

"I'll let you know after I get a look around."

Grange nodded. "It looks like a straightforward case of food poisoning. The call came in to the firehouse about an hour after everybody finished lunch. Gert's body is in the restroom where she was found. Carin is with Norm in the office. They're waiting for you."

"I'll take a look at Gert before I talk to them." Zenobia made a face. "I saw Norm's car out front. I had to park behind him."

Grange smiled. "No comment."

"I better get on with it." She stood up and slung her bag over her shoulder. "Here's hoping we can determine cause of death quickly and get back to the business of fun and games. There's been enough sadness in this town."

"You got that right." Grange rose from behind the desk and tucked his cell phone in his pocket. "I'll walk down with you. I need to stretch my legs. It's going to be a long night. I'm expecting the folks from BCI anytime now. We're going to need their forensic guys to run everything in the kitchen through their lab. We don't have the manpower or the equipment to do it."

"Good luck with that, Pete. I know this bunch can put on a

heck of a spread when there's a party."

"Here you are, Doc." They paused at the door to the ladies room. A uniformed man standing guard held open the door.

"If I can borrow this officer, Pete, I can be out of your hair in two shakes." She smiled up at the serious looking young man. "Care to give me a hand?"

"Deputy?" the sheriff asked.

The officer stood tall and nodded.

Zenobia retrieved blue paper shoe covers from her bag for herself and the deputy. They put on protective gloves and caps and stepped inside.

SEVEN

Velma Gates cursed as she pulled her beat-up Escort into the parking lot at the senior center. The sheriff's car blocked the front walk and two vans sporting 'State Vehicle' license plates sat beside it.

Deputy Moira Potts leaned in Velma's open window. "The center is closed, ma'm."

"It's bingo day," Velma barked. "Can't close."

"I'm sorry, ma'm." Moira tried to hide a smile. "The center is the scene of a—"

"I know. I'm not stupid. I came to play bingo like I do every Wednesday and I ain't leaving 'til I do."

Moira backed away from the car and put her hand on her radio. "Ma'am, someone died here."

Velma nodded. "I heard and I'm real sorry about that. Gert and me used to be friends. We was in Red Hats together. Gert named our group, A *Gaggle of Red Hot Hotties.*" She blew her nose in a man's large handkerchief. "When Ernie died, Big and me brought a bunch of stuff over here for the wake. Yep, I'm gonna sure miss Gert." Velma sniffed. "But, listen here, girlie," her voice grew hard, "it's still bingo day and I came to play. Gert would understand."

While Moira pondered her next move, Velma turned off the ignition and got out of her vehicle. She stepped in front of Moira, her nose even with Moira's belt buckle and her hips stretching beyond the deputy's by a good six inches on either side.

Moira took a step back.

Velma moved with her.

"Are you one of them Amazon women or somethin'?" Velma had to crane her neck back as far as it would go just to see the underside of Moira's chin. "You must be eight feet tall."

Moira threw her shoulders back and looked down at Velma. "I am telling you, ma'm, the center is closed until further notice. The investigation is just getting started and I can't say how long it will take."

Velma reached up as far as her stubby arms would allow and grabbed Moira by the shirtfront. "Listen, you freak. I'm a taxpaying citizen and dues payin' member of this senior citizens center and I WANT TO PLAY BINGO TODAY!"

Sheriff Grange was heading to his cruiser when he spotted Moira and Velma.

"Everything okay, deputy?" he called.

"No, it ain't sheriff," Velma shot back. "This *person* says I can't pay bingo."

The sheriff stuffed his hands in his pockets and ambled over to where the pair stood. He was tired and out of sorts. He missed Amy and was in no mood for anything to do with a member of the Gates clan.

"Mornin', Velma." Grange loosened her grasp from Moira's

shirt. "What's the problem?"

"I came to play bingo like I told *her*. She won't let me in and I'm a member," Velma huffed.

"That's right. The center is closed. No bingo, no mahjong, no poker." Grange had too much on his mind to waste his breath on foolishness. "You need to go home…"

Before he could finish his warning, Velma Gates kicked the sheriff in his brand new knee with one of her little steel-toed boots. She was taking aim at his other knee when Moira dived on top of her crashing Velma, Grange and herself onto the gravel drive.

"Dammit to effing hell," Grange yelled from where he'd landed at the bottom of the pileup. He wriggled free and shook off the women. With a grunt, he managed to roll over and raise himself up onto all fours. The minute he put his weight on the injured knee a lightening bolt of pain shot through his body. He froze, panting, until the stars that flashed before his eyes faded.

Moira regained her footing and offered her boss a hand. "Sheriff, is it…?"

Grange could only nod, as he allowed Moira to help him to his feet. His breathing was rapid and shallow, his face the color of a freshly bleached sheet. He clutched his knee while Velma rolled on her back between his legs like a turtle caught in a fishnet.

"You are under arrest for assaulting a police officer," he yelled down at the squirming woman. It took every ounce of self-control he could muster to resist putting his boot on Velma's stomach. Instead, after a minute's hesitation, he ordered his deputy, "Cuff her, call the office and have them send someone over here to pick her up. *NOW*." He backed away and started to limp back to the building.

Moira hoisted Velma off the ground. "Hands behind your back," she commanded while she struggled to snap on the zip cuffs reserved for over-sized offenders. Once secured, Moira grabbed Velma by the shoulders and shoved the portly perpetrator head first into the back of the cruiser. She slammed the door shut and slumped with her back against the vehicle.

Velma thrashed and yelled and kicked at the window with both feet causing the glass to crack. "I'm gonna sue you two for beatin' up an old lady," she screamed.

"Add destroying government property to the charges, deputy," Grange called from the doorway. He hobbled back to the cruiser and faced his attacker through the cracked glass.

"And, Velma Gates—you are no lady!"

. . .

"What was all that about?" One of the paramedics asked when Grange stormed back inside. "I thought about calling the sheriff," she said with a laugh but stopped with one glare from Grange.

"Damn Gates." He winced as he rubbed his knee. "How's it going in there?" He nodded to the hallway where personnel from the Ohio Bureau of Criminal Investigations loaded plastic bags of items into large coolers. The chests, loaded with the contents of the center's kitchen, would be transported to the agency's labs in London, a suburb of the state capital, Columbus, for analysis.

"Those folks are really efficient. They said they expect to be out of here by late this afternoon. One of the toxicologists said you ought to be able to reopen on Monday."

"I know this seems like overkill, and I've no doubt this was all a bad batch of something or other, but," he swallowed hard before he could continue, "after last year…"

"We have to be sure about what happened." She hoisted the backpack marked 'EMT' onto her slim shoulders.

"Any news on Gert?" he asked.

"Haven't heard. We transferred the last person to University though. Sure hope we aren't looking at any more fatalities."

"Got that right," Grange said. He rubbed his eyes.

"I better get back to the station. Good luck, sheriff." She pushed through the door and sprinted to the waiting ambulance.

Sheriff Grange went into the kitchen where a white clad technician was emptying the refrigerator and cupboards. Two others bagged and labeled each item with where it had been stored down to its placement on a shelf.

"I'll be down the hall in the clinic if you need me," Grange told them. One of the white suits gave him a thumb's up and continued her methodical cataloging.

Grange continued down the hall and stopped at the women's restroom. The door was propped open and one of the BCI team was busy swabbing the toilet seat in the first stall. He looked up when he spotted the sheriff.

"How's it going?" Grange asked.

The technician removed his mask and pointed to the hall. "Let's step out there and talk."

"I'm almost finished here and will do the men's room next. I expect that to go pretty quick so I should be out of your hair in another hour or so."

Grange nodded. "Any ideas on when we'll hear back?"

"I can't say. It could be a week, it could be a month. Just depends." The man rubbed his back. "Once we're done, though, you can reopen. We'll have everything we need when we clear out this afternoon."

"Good. I already had to arrest a disappointed bingo player today. I can only imagine what will happen if we keep folks locked out for long."

"Then I better get on it." The technician grinned. "The thought of an angry mob of senior citizens scares the heck out of me." He replaced his mask and went back to work.

An officer stopped Grange on his way to the clinic. "Dr. Hachett's on the line for you, sheriff."

Grange hurried to the clinic where he'd set up a makeshift command post. "Zenobia? What've you got?"

EIGHT

Hank counted his steps. He'd circled the waiting room in Memorial's emergency department nine times in one thousand, eight hundred and fifty-two steps. In the middle of his tenth turn, he saw Bob Applebee wheel in. Hank stopped counting and sank onto a plastic chair beside his friend.

"Have you heard anything on Tippi or the others? What caused it?" Applebee asked.

Hank shook his head

"Pete finished interviewing everybody who was there and now the forensic people are giving the place a thorough going-over. They told him they'll be done later today and the center can re-open Monday."

"I haven't given my statement yet." Hank watched the door where doctors and nurses emerged then disappeared as friends and families were called into the patient area.

"He knows. He said he'll swing by here after BCI leaves and take care of that."

Mary Schmidt pushed through the doors from the treatment rooms. Her eyes were bloodshot and she appeared confused as she surveyed the waiting area. She clutched a bulging plastic bag.

Hank leaped up and hurried to her side. He put his arm around her waist and gently ushered her to the spot where Applebee waited. "Sit down over here with us."

She collapsed into the seat and looked blankly at the men. She hugged the bag to her chest. "Violet's…," she choked.

"Violet—passed?" Applebee gasped.

"Oh, no, Bob. Not that." Mary looked at him, stricken. "But she's really…" She couldn't go on.

Hank nodded. "We understand, Mary." He unclenched her fingers from the sack and slid it under his chair.

"Can I get you coffee? Water?" He needed to do something.

"Water?" She blinked back tears.

Applebee and Hank exchanged worried looks. When Hank returned with the water, Mary took it and held it in her lap. Applebee took her hands in his and lifted the cup to her mouth. She took a sip and shook her head.

"Violet?" Hank asked.

Mary dabbed her eyes. "They only let me see her for a few minutes. I don't know anything." She looked at the men and a small smile lit up her face. "She opened her eyes when she heard my voice. I squeezed her hand and she squeezed back. It was light but I know I felt it."

"Well, now, that's something." Applebee said.

"That's a good sign, right?" Mary searched her friends' faces for encouragement. "I mean, she knew I was there." She buried her face in Hank's shoulder and sobbed.

A nurse came into the waiting room. She read off an iPad,

"Family for Tabitha Mulgrew?"

Hank called out. "I am. I'm here." He looked at Applebee.

"Go. I've got this." He moved Mary's head to his shoulder.

"Follow me," the nurse said, holding the door. "She's all the way in back." She led Hank through the labyrinth of white-curtained cubicles to one diagonal from the nurse's station. She pulled back the curtain. "The doctor will be in to speak with you shortly," she said brusquely and hurried away.

Hank wiped the tears from his eyes and tried to regain his composure. He stood at the foot of the bed and stared down at the blanketed, still body. Gingerly, he stepped over the wires and tubes that snaked around the bedside.

"I'm here, sweetheart." He fished her hand out from beneath the covers and kissed her forehead.

...

Sheriff Pete Grange stepped into Memorial Hospital's crowded ED waiting room. He removed his hat and pinched the brim in his tired fingers. When he spotted Applebee and Mary Schmidt seated in the far corner, he debated if he should speak to them before getting on with the real reason he was here—a phone call from coroner, Zenobia Hachett.

Zenobia first. He ducked through the door marked *No Admittance.* The hallway on this side led to offices for administrative personnel, doctors' consultations and on a day like this, an area where a small-sized press conference could be held.

Grange recognized a lone reporter from *The Goose Down Daily News* and nodded at the young man. He intended to keep going but stopped when the reporter stepped in front of him.

"Sheriff, can I have a word?"

Grange checked his watch. "Sorry, I gotta go."

"You're meeting with Dr. Hachett, right?"

Grange was about to offer a 'no comment' when Zenobia poked her head out of one the offices and called to him, "Down here, Pete."

"Duty calls."

"If I hang around will you give me the scoop?"

Grange shook his head. "Not tonight. Anything the Doc tells me will have to be confidential until I hear back from BCI. You understand?"

"Yeah." The reporter turned off his recorder and began packing his messenger bag. He held out his hand. "Good luck, Sheriff. I sure hope there's nothing more to the story than a batch of bad brownies."

"Me too." Grange moved toward the office where Zenobia waited. He paused and looked back at the young man. "Tell you what. You'll be the first person I call when I can release the information. Deal?"

"That's a deal, Sheriff. And, thanks."

Sheriff Grange was already halfway down the hall.

...

"Come in and close the door, Pete." The coroner motioned the sheriff to a chair across from her. A thick file sat in the middle of the desk. She took off her glasses and brought out an official-looking report with highlighted sections. She scanned the paper before she looked up.

"Bad news?" Grange asked. The question was a formality. He

hoped his instinct was wrong. He slumped in his chair and waited.

"Yes."

"Better give it to me then."

Zenobia cleared her throat and put her glasses back on. She adjusted them to where they teetered on the end of her nose. "Keep in mind this is still preliminary."

Grange nodded. "Understood."

"Gert had a heart attack."

"What?" The sheriff sat up and leaned forward. "That's good news, right?" He paled and stuttered, "Sorry, that's not…"

"I know what you mean, it's okay." She studied the form, her rings sparkled in contrast to the dark message contained there. "It's what caused the heart attack that has me concerned."

"I don't get it." There was an edge to his voice that he hadn't intended. He took a deep breath and apologized, "Sorry, Doc."

"No need. It's been rough." She handed the report to Grange and pointed to the paragraph highlighted in yellow. "That's the crux of it."

Grange scanned the section the coroner indicated and looked up. He read it again and sat back heavily. "Heart attack caused by acute arsenic poisoning?"

Zenobia nodded. "I became suspicious when I detected the smell of garlic on her so I called the center and asked if anybody remembered if Gert had lunch before becoming ill. BCI told me that garlic bread and lasagna were on the menu that day so that could have explained the odor. Several folks said they remember that Gert wasn't looking well when she arrived that morning, but couldn't say if she ate lunch or not. I got suspicious and rushed the labs."

"I don't know what to say." Grange re-read the report.

"It looks like the poison was building up over time, probably a couple of weeks at least. It must have finally caught up with her yesterday and her body couldn't fight off the effects any longer. We're going to have to check the well on their property. Could be some way the arsenic is seeping into the water. Back in the day, farmers used a lot of arsenic-laden pesticides. It's not used anymore but I'm sure there's still residue that's seeped into the groundwater and probably into the wells of some farms. We're all exposed to low levels of the stuff—apple juice, rice—but at such low levels it doesn't make us sick."

"First, Ernie dies of the flu, then Gert...oh my God. Maybe Ernie...?"

Zenobia shrugged. "That's a good question, Pete. I know his body was cremated but I don't know what Carin and Gert did with his ashes. I have an idea but I hope I'm wrong. If it's what I think, we'll probably never know."

"But how does this explain all those other people getting sick? Tippi? Violet? The others?"

"I don't know yet. It could be something else and it's just a coincidence it all happened on the same day. Botulism is a real possibility with food sitting out for who knows how long. We might be looking at two separate causes here and it could take up to a couple of weeks to get the toxicology reports back. We have to be careful not to jump the gun. Let's take it one step at a time, Pete."

One of the clerks from Registration cracked open the door. 'Carin and Norman Seitz are here to see you, doctor."

Zenobia rose and Grange took it as his cue to leave. He held out his hand. "Thanks for getting back to me so fast, Doc. I imagine you had to call in a few favors for this one."

"Never hurts to keep some in reserve, Pete." She gave him a weak smile. "I'll be in touch."

The sheriff exited the office and barely missed colliding with Norman Seitz pacing the hallway while on his cellphone. Carin was seated on a bench and jumped up to greet him.

"Pete, what's going on? Did Dr. Hachett tell you what happened to Gert?"

"She'll explain everything to you. You have any other questions for me, call my cell—anytime, you hear?"

Norman pocketed his phone and joined his wife.

"Carin, Norm, come in," Zenobia greeted the couple and held the door open.

Grange put on his hat and made his way to the waiting room to speak with Hank and Mary. His day wasn't over yet but the thought of Amy waiting for him at home made what he had to do next a little easier.

NINE

Grange pulled up a seat next to Applebee and Mary. "Any news?"

"Still waiting." Applebee stifled a yawn. "Hank's with Tippi."

"How are you holding up, Mary?" the sheriff asked.

Mary repeated the story of her visit with Violet. "Not knowing is the hardest. I don't know what I'd do if," she fought back tears, "if she doesn't make it. It's just been the two of us since mother passed six years ago."

Applebee squeezed her hand. "We have to think positively, Mary. Right, Pete?"

Grange's mind had drifted and not in a positive direction. He was picturing Zenobia breaking the news to Carin that her stepmother had died of arsenic poisoning and possibly her father as well. This opened up a Pandora's box of possibilities.

"Pete?"

"Sorry." Grange rubbed his knee. There was a knot the size of a golf ball and it hurt like hell.

"What happened?" Applebee pointed to the rust colored blotch of dried blood on the sheriff's pants leg.

"Velma Gates happened."

"Huh?"

"Velma came to play bingo this morning and got a little upset when I told her the center was closed. She's currently in time out over at county."

Applebee chuckled then turned serious. "Was Big Roy cooperative when you interviewed him about..." Applebee glanced at Mary who clung to his arm like a life preserver, "about the, uh, *other* incident?"

"Roy wasn't there."

"He was there. I was playing poker with him. Ate lunch with him too."

"He wasn't there when we did the interviews. Moira made sure nobody left and we made a list of everyone present." Grange paused and said, "Damn. That must have been him I passed when I drove up."

"You know," Applebee chose his words carefully. He pried Mary's hand off of his arm that had fallen asleep under her clutch. "Big Roy didn't eat the lunch. He brought his own food. I remember because we ribbed him about it."

"Interesting." Grange tried to align this new information with what Zenobia had just told him.

"It's hard to forget a grown man choosing Mountain Dew and pork rinds over Arcella's lasagna but he did."

Grange rose and put on his hat. "I guess my day isn't over yet. Damn those Gates." He started to leave when a nurse caught him by the arm.

"Can you hang on a sec, Sheriff?" She inclined her head at Mary and Applebee.

Grange nodded and followed her. She took the seat next to Mary and spoke softly, "Mary, we're going to send Violet to Cincinnati where they're better equipped." She hesitated and looked to Applebee and Grange for support. "Where they have more resources to take care of her." The nurse waited for the news to sink in.

Mary looked at her, uncomprehending. "But our doctor, Dr. Schneider, is here. We never see anyone else. Except for our colonoscopies of course but..."

"Mary," Applebee interrupted, "she's saying Violet needs the kind of care she can't get here. She needs specialists and I'm sure Dr. Schneider understands. Right, nurse?"

"It's Dr. Schneider's orders that she's transferred." The nurse rose to go. "We're getting her ready now. It will be several hours before she'll be settled over there. I suggest you go home and get some rest so you'll be fresh when you see her."

"I'll take you home, Mary. I'll call someone from the center to come stay with you. I would, but Frenchie's been home alone all day and I hate to see what that dog's done to my place." Applebee's smile belied his attempt to sound cross.

"Okay, then," Sheriff Grange stood up and stretched. "I'm going to talk to Big Roy and maybe I'll let Velma out of lockup." He scowled. "I hate to see what *that...*," he hesitated, " that *person,* has done to *my* place."

. . .

Sheriff Grange opened the front door of the station to a wall of Gates. The odor of tobacco mingled with sweaty bodies and damp earth hung in the air like a black cloud.

"Grange, where the hell have you been?" Big Roy's breath reeked of stale beer. "You got a helluva nerve locking up my wife."

"Yeah," Baby joined in. "Police brutality on a senior citizen. We gonna sue your sorry ass."

"Always a pleasure, *gentlemen*—and lady," Grange added, spotting GG on a bench smoking a cigarette. Little Roy stood scowling beside his sister.

The desk sergeant, Ed Waller, waved the sheriff over.

"Excuse me, folks. If you all will have a seat, I'll be with you shortly." Grange stopped in front of GG. "No smoking, Miss."

GG responded by blowing a smoke ring at him.

Grange plucked the stub from her fingers and ground it under the heel of his boot before going to the front desk.

"The inmate give you any trouble, Ed?"

The older man rolled his eyes. "I'd say combat pay is in order, boss."

"Sorry about that." Grange's eyes twinkled. "I need a word with Big Daddy over there then we can get this bunch out of here."

"The charges against the old lady?"

Grange debated the question against the throbbing knot on his knee. "She pays restitution for the cruiser window and I'll drop the charges." He looked back over his shoulder at the family huddled together. "Give me ten minutes, then send Big Roy back. Seems he managed to slip away from the scene on Monday before we could interview him. As much as I'd like to forgo that pleasure, I'm going to have to find out why he left in such a hurry."

...

Thirty minutes later Grange walked Big Roy back to the lobby where the family waited. "Don't plan on leaving the county," he admonished the older man. "This isn't over." He turned on his heel and went back to office, slamming the door behind him.

The sheriff slid behind his desk and slipped off his boots. *Damn Gates. Do I really buy his excuse about leaving the scene because he was running out of air? It's possible.* He dialed his home phone number.

Amy's sleepy voice answered. "Hello?"

"Hey, there. Did I wake you?"

"It's okay."

"Keep my spot warm, okay?" he ended after filling her in on the latest developments.

"You got it, chief," she answered, calling him by the nickname she'd given him on their first date.

TEN

Arcella re-entered the main house after emptying the contents of the refrigerator into the garbage and taking the cans to the road for the next day pick-up. She placed the half-empty bag of hazelnut-flavored coffee left over from Ernie's wake on the top shelf of the cupboard. The couple preferred the coffee sent to them in care packages from family members in San Benito but Arcella couldn't bear the idea of wasting food—or anything for that matter, so she saved this bag for those rare occasions when they had company.

Victor finished locking up and joined his wife in the living room for the eleven o'clock news. The couple sat without speaking as the male and female duo on the screen recounted the news of the day, the focus on the events at the senior center.

Arcella picked up her crocheting from her basket. She was making a baby blanket for her nephew and his wife who were expecting their first child any time now in San Benito. She would finish the blanket with pink or blue ribbons once the baby was born. She held the soft wool against her cheek and prayed for an easy delivery and a healthy baby. She was sad that she would not be present to welcome the newest member to their large family. Sitting here beside her husband of thirteen years, a wave of homesickness washed over her.

"Are you okay?" Victor put his arm around his wife's shoulders.

"What's going to happen to us?"

Victor shook his head. "I don't know."

"What will we do? The money, the house—we're so close." She clutched her husband's sleeve. "Maybe Miss Carin?"

"I don't know." Victor wished he had the words to comfort her but none came. He was worried about their future too and thought about the last time he'd spoken to his boss, a man whom he'd thought of as his friend. They were in the barn stacking bales of hay when he asked Ernie about purchasing five acres from him to build a house for himself and Arcella. Ernie told him that would be impossible since he intended to place the land under a trust with CLAW that included a clause agreeing to preserve the property as is and disallowing any new building on the site. He added that their farm was home to several endangered species, including a certain crayfish that lived in their pond. When Victor heard that he lost his temper. He'd lit into him, let loose a string of expletives in Spanish and flatly accused Ernie of exploiting their immigration status by using him and Arcella as cheap labor. He hurled a hay bale at his employer and hit the older man squarely in the chest knocking him to the ground. Victor said he quit and stormed out.

Afterward, he told his wife he had to go into town on an errand and spent the rest of the afternoon knocking back Dos Equis' at *El Gris Ganso.* Later, Victor told his wife it was true what they say about when one door closes, another one opens.

While Victor was drowning his sorrows in beer, Big Roy Gates had wandered in and asked if he could join him for a drink. Victor, who was pretty well inebriated by then, began to relate the story about his fight with Ernie, his dream of owning his own home and how everything he thought possible when coming to America had been destroyed. "All because Schwab and those damn CLAWs think some damn fish is more important than a human being. I don't give a damn if that's the last damn fish in the whole stinking country."

Big Roy told him he understood totally. He motioned to the bartender to bring another round and when they'd been served, he leaned his head back and drained his beer. He wiped his mouth on his sleeve before he said, "You've heard the saying 'where's there's a will, there's a way'?"

Victor shook his head 'no' and waited.

"What it means is—I think I can help."

...

Arcella tucked the baby blanket into the basket. She waited for Victor in the small sitting room of the tiny guesthouse where they'd lived since first coming to manage the farm.

"How about a walk before we turn in?" Victor asked his wife when he'd finished securing the house.

"Okay. I don't think I can sleep anyway." Arcella offered him a weak smile as he arranged her shawl across her shoulders.

Their cottage was situated on the next rise beside a pond where a flashing orange beacon floated to keep away the geese that liked to use the area as a nesting ground. A pair of trumpeter swans patrolled the water. Victor shone the flashlight down the flagstone steps and around the patch of yard Arcella had planted with flowers, vegetables and herbs. The fragrance of basil mingled with ripe tomatoes floated like a mist around them.

The couple strolled hand-in-hand across the property as chirping insects and frogs sang to one another. They walked at a leisurely pace, unconcerned as crime in this part of the county was mostly confined to kids riding around the country roads on Saturday nights taking out mailboxes with baseball bats.

"It's so pretty out," Arcella said when they came back inside. "I love it when the sky is clear and there's only a sliver of moon. The stars look so bright."

"Want to sit on the porch for a while?" Victor asked. He held her close in an embrace and was about to kiss her when he pulled away. He moved to the window and peered into the darkness.

"What is it? What's wrong?" Arcella moved behind him and stood on tiptoe to see over his shoulder.

"I don't know. I thought I saw something over by the barn. Probably just a deer." He moved away and lifted his shotgun down from the rack above the door. "Just in case, I'm going to take a look. People know the Schwabs are—aren't here." He swallowed hard. "Somebody might be up to mischief. I doubt it but I'll check just to be sure."

"Do you want me to come with you?" Arcella worried.

"No, just keep an eye out from here." He kissed her forehead. "I'm sure it's nothing."

Victor checked to make sure the gun was loaded then hefted the gun-strap over his shoulder. He picked up the flashlight and let himself back out into the cool dark night.

As he neared the barn, he could make out the silhouette of a pickup. A man's figure in dark pants and hoodie hoisted a ladder into the bed of the truck where someone waited to take it from him. The man on the ground disappeared back inside. The figure in the truck lit a cigarette.

As Victor crept closer, he recognized Baby Roy Gates emerging with Ernie's chainsaw. He swung his light onto the hulking figure in the truck. It was Little Roy.

"Hold it right there," Victor yelled. "What do you two think you're doing?"

When he spotted Victor, Baby pulled the starter rope and fired up the saw. "Wanna see a Mex-ee-can-ee bean jump, brother?" He cackled and moved toward Victor, swinging the saw in front of him.

"Turn that off and put it down *now,*" Victor commanded. He set the flashlight on the ground and with his right hand, removed the gun from his shoulder and took aim. He kept his gun-sight on Baby who continued to move toward him swinging the chainsaw.

Little Roy groaned as he jumped out of the pickup, hitting the ground with a thud. Once he got his balance, he reached into his pocket and brought out a book of matches. He lit the match and touched it to an object he cradled in his other hand.

A sudden flash of light and a loud explosion threw Victor off balance. As he stumbled backward, his finger hit the trigger. The last thing he remembered was Baby's scream and the chainsaw sputtering across the grass.

ELEVEN

When Hank returned to the waiting area, he was surprised to find Applebee still there. "Hey, I thought you'd be gone."

"I'm on my way, but I wanted to catch you before I left." He motioned for Hank to sit down. "Moira Potts stopped by to get an update and when I told her about Violet, she offered to take Mary home and spend the night with her. She'll drop her off at the hospital in the morning on her way to work." He wheeled around to face his friend. "How's Tippi?"

"Not good. The doctor is trying to get her stabilized." Hank ran his fingers through his hair.

"The evidence tech from BCI asked us about everything we'd eaten since arriving at the center. I only had some salad and an apple since Doc Schneider told me to lose weight. He said if I didn't, I'd be needing the jaws-of-life to get me out of this chair." Applebee sighed and patted his paunch. "Those brownies were awful tempting."

"I guess we both lucked out though I didn't think so then. By the time I got through the line, the vultures had cleaned out the place."

"Uh oh, now what?" Applebee turned when a red pick-up screeched to a halt at the ED entrance.

The men saw Little Roy Gates swing open the driver's side door and waddle around to the back of the truck. He leaned inside and hoisted Baby's limp body over his shoulder. Hank ran outside to assist but by then a nurse hurried forward with a wheelchair. Hank and the nurse lifted Baby from his brother's shoulders and the three of them managed to shove him into the chair.

The nurse, followed by Little Roy, wheeled Baby through the onlookers clustered around the door.

A beat-up Escort squealed to a stop behind the truck. Velma Gates wriggled her round little body out of the driver's seat and hurried around to the passenger's side where Big Roy struggled to stand up. He leaned on the car door for support and swore at his wife as she bent to untangle the plastic tubing that tethered him to the tank.

"Anybody in there wanna help me?" Velma screamed.

Hank glanced at Applebee who shrugged. He rose wearily from his seat and went back outside. "Need a hand, Velma?"

"No, genius. We're just putting' on a show for all you losers with nothin' better to do." She yanked at the tubing as she talked.

"Let me," Hank said. He managed to free Big Roy's legs while Velma stood by cursing. "What happened?"

"Baby's been shot. Dead. Murdered in cold blood," Velma shouted. She hoisted the oxygen tank onto her shoulder and barreled toward the door.

"Slow down, old woman." The tubing, pulled taut in Roy's nose, acted like a leash as he trotted behind trying to keep pace.

"There's going be two dead Gates before the night's out if you don't hold up," he wheezed.

Big Roy passed the oxygen tank to Little Roy who lumbered behind his parents. He motioned for him to follow him to the treatment area where a nurse held the door. "Wait here, Vel," Big Roy commanded his wife.

Velma turned a tear-streaked face to Hank.

"Baby was murdered?" Hank couldn't believe what he was hearing. *Could this day get any worse?*

"Yeah," she sniffed, "and it was that Mexican that done it."

...

Norman and Carin joined Hank and Applebee in time to hear the story of Baby's murder. According to Velma, the family had just gotten back from the police station when Baby and Little Roy noticed some 'funny stuff' at Ernie's place. Being the good neighbors they were, Velma said, they decided to take a ride over for a 'look-see'.

"They thought maybe it was them CLAWs back again and up to no good," Velma huffed.

Big Roy emerged from the treatment area. He gingerly lowered himself into a seat next to Applebee. He caught Norm's eye before he looked at his wife, who despite her grief, was clearly enjoying herself as the center of attention.

"They wuz checking in the barn when that damn Mexican walked up and shot Baby. For doin' nothin' 'cept trying to help." Velma wiped a tear from her eye and looked around to determine the impact on the group.

Big Roy cleared his throat. "Um, you all can understand how

the boy's mother is upset." He turned to his wife. "Fact is, Baby's alive." He thrust his chin forward and looked around, defying anyone to challenge him. "Baby got cut with the saw defending himself when the Mexican snuck up on him with a gun and he passed out. He'll need a few stitches in his, uh," he coughed, "in his, uh, leg." His face reddened.

Applebee covered his face with his hands, his body heaved with silent laughter.

"But what was Baby doing...?" Hank wrinkled his forehead trying to picture the scene.

"What are you suggesting, Klaber? Just because my boy had a run in or two with the law... " Big Roy bellowed, his face scarlet with rage.

"Now, Roy," Norm squatted down next to him. "I can speak for all of us when I say we're real glad to hear Baby's going to be okay. Right, guys?"

Heads nodded and muffled voices of 'yeses' and 'you bets' ended the discussion.

"Now, I'm going to take Carin home," Norm said, gripping his hand, "and put her to bed. She's had a helluva day. Once she's settled, I'll give you a call, Roy, to check on Baby, you know. That okay?" Norm clapped him on the shoulder and squeezed hard as he stood up.

"Okay." Roy twisted away from the younger man's grip and rubbed his shoulder.

"Let's go, Carin." Norman headed for the door. His wife followed behind him.

"Hank Klaber?" A nurse stood in the door and looked around

the room.

"Right here." Hank hurried forward.

The nurse motioned him to follow her to the nurse's station in back where he was met by Doctor Schneider. "Let's step over here, Hank." He led Hank to a corner of the room out of the way of the nurses, technicians and hospital personnel hustling in and out of treatment rooms. The doctor looked tired. "We have some preliminary results back from Tippi's lab work and I've also been in touch with Zenobia."

"What is it, Doc?"

"Arsenic poisoning."

"What? How's that possible? How...?"

"Like I said, this is early, but I've seen it before. After consulting with Zenobia, I requested blood cell counts and serum electrolyte labs on everybody to be certain."

"But Doc, if the tests all come back...do you think that means...?" He couldn't bring himself to say the words.

"I can't say anymore, Hank. But, for right now," he wiped his hand across his forehead, "right now her condition is critical and I want to send her to University Hospital."

"But she's going to be okay, right, Doc?"

"I'd say if you're a praying man, Hank, this is the time."

TWELVE

Sheriff Grange was looking forward to catching a couple hours of sleep. It had been a long and difficult day and the thought of climbing into bed beside Amy, even for a quick nap, offered some comfort. He was pulling into his garage when his radio crackled.

"Sheriff," the desk sergeant's voice came in strong, "I'm sorrier than hell about this, but you're needed back at Memorial. Baby Gates has been in an altercation with Victor Alvarez."

"Oh, jeez. Anybody dead?" Grange asked, half joking.

"Thought so at first but, no, they're both alive."

"Holy crap, I only left them an hour ago. How could he have gotten into trouble already? That's a record even for a Gates'."

"If it's any consolation, you'll get a kick out of the story. Better hurry though. Hospital security has Baby detained and Mom and Pop are making a helluva scene.""

"I just got home. I'm gonna run inside and change my shirt and grab a sandwich. I'll be over there in two shakes."

"Roger that." The radio went silent.

...

The sheriff finished the last of his peanut butter and jelly sandwich as he eased the cruiser into the hospital parking spot designated for emergency personnel. He straightened the brim of his uniform hat and put it on. He sipped from the thermos of coffee Amy had made him, tucked it under his arm and stepped out.

"'Bout time, Grange," Velma Gates greeted him as he approached the entrance. "Them Mexicans almost killed my Baby and you stopped for lunch?" she exploded, eying the thermos.

"Good evening to you too, Velma." Grange tried to sound civil but he was worn out and another encounter with the Gates family stretched his patience nearly to breaking.

"I want you to lock up that damn killer, Sheriff. And then I want you to ship him and that wife 'a his back to Ti-ja-wann-a or whatever the hell place they come from."

"First of all, Velma, Baby's alive, so nobody's a killer. Secondly, I'm going to talk to Baby," he said. He walked to the doors leading to the patient area. "Alone," he added when she started to follow him inside. "Then, when I'm through, I'll decide what to do. Got it?"

"No, I don't. He's my boy and..."

Grange turned and placed a hand on Velma's shoulder. "I know you had a bad scare tonight, Velma, and I promise, I'll get to the bottom of this, okay?"

Velma nodded through real tears this time.

The sheriff looked down at the pinched, little face and went inside.

...

Grange finished his interviews with Baby and Little Roy and decided he couldn't put off talking to Victor. It was already three a.m. and he needed to catch a few hours of sleep but the job always came first.

Hank was seated in the empty waiting room. He looked up when the sheriff approached. "Heading home, Pete?"

Grange shook his head. "Not yet." He gave Hank a weak smile. "I beginning to think I'm getting too old for this job. Between the goings on at the center and dealing with the Gates', I feel like I died and woke up in…"

Hank grimaced.

"Sorry, buddy." He put on his hat and glanced up at Hank. "Everything okay, Hank? How's Tippi?"

Hank tried to answer but the words stuck in his throat. He shook his head and stared down at his shoes.

"They're getting her ready to transfer to University. It's bad, Pete, really bad."

...

Victor and Arcella Alvarez sat across from Sheriff Grange at their kitchen table. A chipped plate with brownies sat in front of him.

"Coffee, Sheriff?" Arcella asked. "When you called, I made a fresh pot. Hazelnut." She filled up an oversized mug with the steaming liquid. "What's going to happen to Victor?" Her voice trembled.

The sheriff added two heaping spoonfuls of sugar and a generous splash of milk to his coffee. He tucked the small notebook he'd used for notes into his shirt pocket and helped himself to a brownie. He bit into the creamy chocolate and washed it down with a long drink.

"Your stories match up for the most part with Baby's and Little

Roy's," Grange said. "Except for their reason for being in Ernie's barn in the first place, of course—and the part about Little Roy setting off that firecracker." Grange dabbed his mouth with the napkin Arcella offered him. "I mean, who carries firecrackers around in their pockets? Jeez."

"Are you going to arrest my husband, sheriff?"

"No, Ma'am. Those boys were up to no good as evidenced by having possession of Ernie's ladder and chainsaw. I'm pretty sure I can convince them the only real case here is against them for trespassing and attempted theft. I'll write up the report tomorrow and Victor, you will need to come down to the station to sign it. That should wrap it up." He rose to go. "Now I'm going home to catch some shut-eye for whatever is left of this night and I suggest you two do the same."

"For the trip home." Arcella emptied the remainder of the coffee into the thermos the sheriff had brought inside with him. "Another brownie for the road?"

"I never say no to your baking, Mrs. A." He grinned and wrapped the chocolate in his paper napkin.

...

Grange backed the cruiser away from the cottage and took his time making his way down the long gravel driveway with its twists and turns before arriving at the state route that bordered Ernie's farm. He swung onto the empty road and turned toward town and the tidy brick bungalow he'd lived in since he'd carried his teenage bride, Ivy, over the threshold thirty odd years ago. When she died of pancreatic cancer two years ago, Grange assumed he would spend the rest of his life alone. He learned, as his pastor liked to say, "Man plans and God laughs," and Amy Spencer came into his life when he stopped her for driving fifty-five in a thirty mile per hour zone. She'd looked up at him with big blue eyes and thick brown lashes and the sheriff was a goner. He wrote out her ticket and then invited her to dinner.

The sheriff took a long pull from the thermos. Fatigue and drowsiness overtook him and the vice that had begun to clamp itself around his head grew tighter with each mile. He popped Arcella's brownie into his mouth in hopes the sugar would jolt him awake. Instead, his stomach cramped so fiercely he thought he was going to have to pull over. He clung to the steering wheel and inched the cruiser along through the empty streets.

Made it. He breathed a sigh of relief when he pulled into his driveway and punched the button on the garage door opener. As he started to ease the vehicle forward, a spasm wrenched his gut so hard he pitched forward, his seat belt clamping tightly across his chest and the air bag muffling the sound of the cruiser's bumper as it sliced into the steel tool cabinet on the back wall of the garage.

THIRTEEN

Norman Seitz greeted the young couple at the door to his office and ushered them inside. The conference room was comfortably furnished with a gleaming mahogany table and six high-backed chairs of soft, brown leather. The side walls were lined with photographs of Norm with lesser-known celebrities mixed among awards and membership plaques from local civic organizations. One very large photo of him standing in front of Fowler Towers, the tallest building in Goose Down at six stories and the centerpiece of the Main Street business district, was displayed on the wall behind his chair at the head of the table. In the photo, Norm held two certificates signed by Bobo Fowler himself, proclaiming Norman Seitz a graduate of the Fowler University College of Realtors, F.U.C.R. and Fowler University College of Underwriters, F.U.C.U.

He pretended to straighten the certificates in their ornate gold frames on the opposite wall. Once he was satisfied his guests were duly impressed, he sat down and waved them to take seats on either side of him. He made a show of straightening the stack of papers laid out for the meeting before offering each of them

Mont Blanc pens matching his own.

"May I have my assistant bring you something to drink?" he asked the man first then directed his question to the woman. "Coffee, water, perhaps a soft drink?"

"I could use some water, thanks," the man answered. "Jackie?" he asked his wife.

She shook her head and nervously twisted the pen in her fingers. Her nails were ragged and bitten to the quick and the gold plated band she wore was chipped exposing a glint of hard steel.

Norm's new assistant, a temp, brought in several bottles of water stamped with the words *Money Matters, LLC*.

"Are you ready to buy a house?" Norm asked.

Jackie clasped her husband's hand. Worry lines creased her forehead.

"We are," William answered. He gently placed his wife's hand in her lap. "Let's do it." He sat up tall and looked Norm squarely in the eye.

Norm went through the process of outlining the terms of the purchase agreement before passing the forms, one by one, for signing. He patiently explained the purpose of every one and asked each time if they understood. It was a process he'd repeated many times in recent weeks however he was careful to treat each transaction as though it were unique. He wanted his buyers to feel special—and they always did.

Now comes the tricky part. "I believe you have something for me?" Norm said, with a half-grin.

William handed Norm the cashier's check for ten thousand dollars the couple borrowed from Jackie's father for the down payment and a second, personal check, for two thousand dollars.

"And, since we aren't dealing with those crooks some people call bankers, we've avoided all the hidden fees, inspection costs and the like," Norm said, waving his hand dismissively, "by keeping this just between us."

"Can you explain something to us again, Mr. Seitz?" William said. "Jackie and me still don't get why you called and needed this additional two thousand dollars?"

"No problem," Norm said. He took a deep breath and studied the file in front of him. "I do this every day so I forget the legal mumbo-jumbo isn't what most people—even smart people like yourselves—are familiar with. Lawyers, right?" Norm laughed.

William nodded to his wife.

"Okay. Since you are purchasing the property directly from me, what's called in the business as 'seller financed', I have what's known as an 'insurable interest'. Essentially, I need to be able to cover my expenses, advertising, improvements, you know, all the money I've invested in the place. Unfortunately, it turned out that the house needed more work than I estimated when we first spoke. " He looked downcast, then smiled. The request for more money came when Norm decided he needed to move up his timeline and put the squeeze on his 'clients' wherever he could. He planned to be long gone by the end of the month and safely beyond the long arm of the law.

"Okay, I guess," William said. "I think I've got it." He looked to his wife. "We good, hon?"

Jackie beamed at her young husband and nodded.

"Smart girl." Norm interrupted. "She's a keeper, Willy." He

shuffled through the stack of papers in front of him. "Oops, forgot the most important one. Hang on." He went to his desk and retrieved a folder labeled 'New Deeds' that he kept on file, notarized and signed. "All set. Now, let's get you a house."

Norm hurried the pair through the rest of the forms and when they were finished, he used the intercom to call his assistant. "We're all done in here." He turned to William. "We'll get your deed recorded and send copies of all the paperwork to you. We'll handle everything—don't worry. All you need to do now is take this pretty little wife of yours out to dinner to celebrate," Norm said warmly as he held out a hand first to Jackie then to William. "I know you'll be very happy in your new home—and you got a fantastic deal."

William rose to leave and started to put the pen into his coat pocket.

"Oops, sorry, old man, I'll need those back." Norm held out his hand to a red-faced William and turned to Jackie for hers.

...

Big Roy Gates sat with his nose in a thick book, *Crime and Punishment*. He looked up as the couple entered and bookmarked the page.

"Come on in, Roy." Norm held open the door to his office. "Need a hand?"

"Naw. I'm used to lugging this damn air around," Big Roy said as he got to his feet. He tucked his book under one arm and with the other, wheeled the oxygen tank into place beside the chair offered him.

Roy sat across from Norm, the wide desk empty now except

for an ice bucket, a two-liter bottle of Mountain Dew and a tall glass of ice. A MacBook and a laser printer sat on the credenza. A picture of Norm with Carin and Sauerkraut on the beach in Cancun appeared in the background. Roy placed his book in front of him.

Norm raised his eyebrows. "That's what I'd call heavy reading," he joked, hefting the book with two hands.

"Funny," Roy said taking the book and placing it on the floor next to his chair.

Norm pointed to the soda.

Roy nodded. He waited as Norm poured him a drink, then took a long swallow, after which he wiped his mouth on his sleeve.

"Have you talked with those guys from CLAW?" Norm asked.

"I put a call in to them the night old lady Schwab—oh, sorry," he said, remembering the recently deceased was Norm's mother-in-law. "I mean Miz Schwab, passed. I haven't heard back."

"Have you talked with Velma about my offer?"

"I don't need Velma's permission. I'm the man and I make the decisions. The Gates' are not a democracy." Big Roy emptied his glass and pushed it across the desk for a refill.

Norm rose from his seat and went to the window. The view of rolling hills and farms always made him smile. He stood with his hands clasped behind him and rocked back on the heels of his new Ferragamo loafers. "You know what I see when I look out there, Big Roy?" He didn't wait for an answer. "I see houses, lots of houses. I see condos, apartment buildings, even a golf course."

"Humph, I see nothing but corn and soybeans with some cows and hogs stinking up the neighborhood." Roy's wheezy cackle sounded like wind screeching through a rotten window frame. "I think you must be hallucinating."

Norm sat down. "That's called vision, Roy." He leaned back and clasped his hands behind his head. "Remember that when you talk to those tree-huggers at CLAW. I got a call in to Walmart about building on the site too so don't screw this up."

"I hear you." Big Roy stood up and wheeled his oxygen tank around the chair. He retrieved his book and said, "You got my list? I've only got forty-five minutes left on this tank. I have to get home."

Norm opened the top drawer and pulled out two thick manila envelopes. He slid the packets across the desk. One folder was labeled 'Insurance', the other read 'Property'. "End of the week, Roy. I may be gettin' prettier but I'm not gettin' any younger." He swiveled his chair around so he was facing the window. "I should have your money soon."

...

Norm took two more files from his drawer. He studied each carefully before turning to his computer. He launched the Internet browser and checked his email before opening Craigslist. He scanned in photos from one of the files to add two new listings to Goose Down 'For Sale; seller financed'.

Next, he launched the obituary sections of the *Cincinnati Enquirer* and *The Goose Down Daily News.* He looked through the columns of recent deaths. *Guess my investments haven't paid off yet. He* copied and pasted several new notices into a file on his computer. *Gotta love a grieving widow.* He opened Excel, checked his spreadsheet and added today's payment to September's receipts. He frowned at the result. *I'm really going to have to step up my game.*

The young assistant knocked and stepped inside.

Norm hit 'sleep' and the screen went dark.

"I'm all through here. Anything you need before I go?"

"No thanks. I won't be far behind." He followed her to the door.

"I'm sorry about your mother-in-law. That must be rough."

She was about to leave when the office phone rang. Before she could answer, Norm picked up. He placed his hand over the receiver. "I got it. You go on home."

"Seitz here."

FOURTEEN

Sheriff Grange stirred. His eyelids felt heavy when he strained to force them open. Warm, moist air reeking of tuna fish blew over his face. His stomach churned as he fought back the bile rising in his throat.

"I think he's waking up."

A hand grabbed his shoulder and shook him. "Pete," a second voice shouted in his ear. "Hey, sheriff, it's us—Wittekind and Elrod. You're in the hospital." Mr. Wittekind spoke from the other side of the bed.

"We're right next door." Elrod Klienfelter leaned into Grange's ear and spoke in a voice so loud one of the corpses downstairs in the morgue shuddered, "Your lunch is here—meatloaf, mashed..."

Grange's stomach lurched and his eyes sprung open in time to see Elrod's fingertip, frosted with potato waving before him.

"You want this?" He offered the finger to Grange.

The sheriff's eyes drifted shut. He wanted nothing more than to fall back into the dreamless sleep that someone—or something—was attempting to keep him from.

Mr. Wittekind leaned over and poked the sheriff's cheek with his thumb. "I had the tuna casserole," he offered. "Darn good."

Grange opened one eye. *Am I dreaming or is this what hell is like?"*

"You gonna eat this chocolate pudding, sheriff? If not..." Elrod held up a cup of brown glop under Grange's chin.

"Nurse!" Grange exploded. He searched the covers for a call button. "Damn it! Somebody get in here, *now*!"

"I'm on it, Sheriff." Elrod slid off the bed and hurried to the door. His hospital gown barely met at his sides giving anyone standing, or in the sheriff's case, laying, in back of him, a full view of his backside, wrinkled, sagging buttocks and more.

"For God's sake, man, do a dying man a favor—AND COVER YOUR ASS!" Grange sat up and rattled the side rails on the bed that were preventing his escape.

A nurse, followed by Elrod, pushed a cart with a computer on it into the room. "Hello, boys. I see you're all getting back to normal."

Mr. Wittekind, who at least had the decency to wear boxers splashed with giant red lips under his gown, decided to turn on the charm. "It's only because of your excellent care nurse Kathy that we are beginning to feel the fullness of our manhood return. Why, a few more days under your care—and let me not forget the outstanding work of the kitchen staff—and my friends and I—did I mention I'm a bachelor? My friends and I will be good as new." He reached to pat Nurse Kathy's bottom and was stopped when she grabbed his arm and wrested it behind his back.

"Now, now, *Bernie*."

Mr. Wittekind gasped at her strength.

"If I let go and don't *accidentally* break your arm, are you going to be a gentleman, *Bernie?*"

Mr. Wittekind blushed crimson and nodded.

"You two fellas let me and the sheriff have some privacy now and I'll see if I can't rustle up some ice cream when I'm through. Deal?"

Mr. Wittekind rubbed his arm as he left the room. Elrod followed. He made an unsuccessful attempt to hold the back of his gown together.

"Interesting company you keep, Sheriff." Kathy slipped on the blood pressure cuff on him and clicked entries into her computer. She finished and called back over her shoulder as she strode to the door, "You were lucky, sheriff. You dodged a bullet this time."

. . .

The sun was coming up as Deputy Moira Potts opened the back door of the cruiser and stood aside. She waited for Arcella and Victor Alvarez to climb in and secure their seat belts. She saw Victor take his wife's hand and hold it tightly on the seat between them. Arcella looked terrified. Moira resisted the temptation to tell her everything was going to be all right—that was something she was afraid might not be true.

By the time they arrived at the station, Arcella was shaking so badly, Victor and Moira had to help her inside. The deputy ushered the woman into one of the interview rooms and offered to get her a bottle of water before shutting her inside.

"Can't I stay with her?" Victor asked Moira. "She's so scared."

"I'm sorry, Mr. Alvarez. It's policy." Moira opened the door to the second interview room and pulled out a chair. "You'll need to wait in here and someone will be with you shortly." Moira started to leave but turned around. "I'll keep checking on her."

...

As soon as Ed hung up the phone, it rang again. This had been going on since the news broke about the scene at the senior citizens center. He took a deep breath, counted to five and answered the next call.

"Grange here," the sheriff's familiar voice came through the line.

"Sheriff. How are you?" The sergeant's voice was grave.

"I'm better. Still at Memorial. If I don't get out of here soon, I'm going to be looking at one of our cells from the inside."

Ed chuckled. "Giving the staff a hard time, are you?"

"The other way around. The other way around." The sheriff's voice took on a sober tone. "Fill me in. Where are we?"

"Moira picked up the Alvarezes this morning. We have them in interrogation but haven't taken their statements yet. I phoned BCI and their forensics team will be back down first thing in the morning."

"Doc Schneider will be here soon and I'm demanding my release. I'll come straight to the station."

"We're managing this, Pete. Sit tight for one more day and do what the doc tells you. Moira's is preparing to take statements."

"No. I will handle this. I'll be there this afternoon if I have to sign myself out."

His sergeant sighed. He and Grange had worked together a long time. He knew when he could and when he could not win an argument with the sheriff.

"Right, boss."

...

Sheriff Grange closed the door to the interview room behind him. Exhaustion was etched in his face. Deputy Potts met him in the hallway and took his arm.

"Sheriff, you need to go home. Amy is in your office and we're losing the battle to keep her from storming in and taking you out of here by the ear."

Grange nodded. "I give up. Tell her I'll be there in a minute." He rubbed his forehead and said, "Deputy, take Victor and Arcella home and help them collect some clothes and personal items. I've already checked with Father at St. Mathias and he offered to find a family in the parish to put them up for a few days. BCI will be arriving at their place in the morning."

Moira nodded. "Will do, sheriff. Anything else?"

Grange rubbed his eyes and covered his face before he looked back at his deputy. "Have them hand over their papers."

FIFTEEN

Norman Seitz sat in his office, staring out at the landscape below him. He'd given his assistant, the week off. This close-knit community was still reeling from Gert's death. The young woman had been a member of Gert's Sunday school class and the news hit her hard. Norm was happy to give her the time since he was conducting less and less legitimate business and it was getting difficult to hide his 'other', albeit more lucrative transactions, from her.

Norm's cell rang. When he saw who the call was from, he debated letting it go to voice mail. "Damn." He was in no mood for this conversation. Norm hesitated before he answered, "Good morning." He drew a sharp breath and listened to the voice on the line. "Hmm, I understand." He swiveled his chair around toward his desk and rubbed his temple as the voice on the other end droned on. "All right. This afternoon. I'll bring a check ...A credit card—fine." He ended the call without waiting for a response.

He turned on his laptop then unlocked his file drawer to retrieve a manila file folder. He hit the second number on speed dial while he flipped through the file contents.

"Yeah?" Big Roy growled. A television blared in the background.

"Did you check out that list of properties I gave you?"

"It's drying' up out there but there's one that would work. Good thing you're expanding the business."

"All eggs, one basket. Yada, yada, yada. You keep mining the senior center, I'll work the obits. I'd like to get out of the real estate biz all together. Those damn CLAWs are killing me."

"Hmmm. Okay." Roy paused. "Anyway, if you want the file, you'll have to come out to pick it up. I got somebody coming by this afternoon."

"Okay." The hairs on the back of Norm's neck rose. He and Big Roy had an understanding—they trusted each other—not at all.

"I have to run out to SunDown Ridge in about an hour. I can stop by after."

Big Roy cackled so hard he had a coughing fit. When he finally got his breath, he wheezed, "I had a visit with that old SOB yesterday. I like to stay in touch. We're cousins, you know."

"Right. Real close. Anyway, what could you two possibly have to talk about? You placin' bets with the old man's bookie for 'im?"

"Something like that," Roy said.

"Be a shame if you happened to *accidentally* drop a pillow over his face for three or four minutes." Norm said.

"Real nice."

"Maybe one day soon I'll be seeing you both at the Ridge. Unless, of course, you blow yourself up smoking and huffing on that tank of yours. Velma won't have anything left to bury. She can just vacuum you up."

"Velma, vacuum? That's rich." The line went dead.

Norm turned back to the screen on his laptop. He searched through his files until he found what he was looking for. He studied the contents, then punched a number into his cell phone.

He was about to hang up when a woman's voice answered.

"Mrs. Vaccaro?"

"Yes."

"May I speak to Mr. Vaccaro, please?"

Silence, a sniffle, then, "My husband passed five days ago. Who's calling?"

"Oh, dear. I'm so sorry." Norm referred to his file. "I'm calling about your husband's life insurance policy. I should probably call back later."

"No, wait. Did you say insurance?" Mrs. Vaccaro's voice changed. "I wasn't aware—I mean I didn't know Charlie had life insurance. He always said he didn't believe in it. We were never blessed with children, so," more sniffles, "I'm just surprised, that's all."

"Maybe he knew he was sick?"

"Oh, no, Charlie wasn't sick. He was kicked in the head by a horse he was shoeing over in Trenton. He never regained consciousness."

"I see. Well, sometimes folks change their minds about insurance. He must have done that because he took out a policy for two-hundred thousand dollars from my company several years ago."

"Two hundred-thousand dollars? I can't believe it. Are you sure you have the right Charlie, I mean, Charles Vaccaro?"

"Well, let's just make sure. Can you confirm your address?"

Mrs. Vaccaro supplied the information.

"Now, I need to verify Mr. Vaccaro's birthdate." Norm read off the date recorded in the obituary that the deceased man's wife confirmed.

"One last thing then we can proceed with processing your claim." Norm paused. He crunched some paper into the handset for Mrs. Vaccaro's benefit. "I need you to verify your husband's social security number."

"Hold on, I'll get it." The woman returned with the information.

Norm smiled to himself. *This is almost too easy.*

"Got it, thanks. Now before we can send you your money, as I said at the outset, there is a tiny problem with your husband's claim. However," he added before she could interrupt, "we can easily fix this." He rustled some more papers for effect. "It seems your husband had fallen slightly behind on his premiums. Um, this is awkward, but were you and Charlie having some financial difficulties that may have caused this? I have to ask because if we can show financial hardship as the cause, we can easily rectify the problem by catching you up with the payments so you can collect your two-hundred thousand dollars." Norm used the payout number as bait when performing this operation. So far, it always worked.

"Oh, dear. Now, don't misunderstand, because Charlie worked hard all his life. But a few years ago, when the economy got so bad, Charlie lost his job at the pillow factory."

Norm remembered when *Down to Sleep,* the town's largest

employer, laid off several hundred workers during what politicians referred to as an 'economic downturn'.

"That's when he turned to working as a farrier, something he'd done as a teenager. It wasn't much but it kept a roof over our heads. We were lucky because we had the farm so we could still keep food on the table. Even so, it was two years before he got called back to the factory. It was just this past year before we started to get caught up." She sniffled. "He was going to give up shoeing when he had the accident. He said it was a job for a young man."

"You can at least be thankful your Charlie was looking out for you by having insurance. I tell you what, I'll put through this request for a hardship case as the reason for the lapse in payment. We should be able to submit your claim as soon as we get you caught up with those missed payments."

"Sir?" Mrs. Vaccaro said. "I'm sorry, I didn't get your name."

"Quite alright, Ma'am. Any questions? I'm sorry but I have a call coming in from the insurance company."

"Do you know how much I'll have to pay?"

"I'll let you know the exact number but, I estimate around ten thousand."

"That much?"

"Yes, but you are talking about a two-hundred thousand dollar payout. Sometimes people use their house as collateral?" He let the idea sink in.

"I guess I could do that."

"I have to go, Mrs. Vaccaro, but I'll be in touch." Norm was thinking he might be able to raise the stakes if the old bat had enough equity in the farm.

"Thank you for everything— Mr.?"

Norm stayed on the line as he went into the conference room. "Gates. Roy Gates with Money Matters. Oops, gotta run. Yep, this is Charlie's company on the other line. Hold on."

Norm paused in front of the portrait of himself standing beside Bobo Fowler. Still on the line, he tugged at one side of the frame. He swung open the picture to reveal a wall safe. He riffled through the contents until he found what he wanted—the Ruger LCP.

"Oh, ma'am?" he said, before he hung up, "I'm sorry for your loss."

...

The cloying odor of lemon and decay assaulted Norm's senses the minute he stepped into the lobby of SunDown Ridge Extended Care. He wrinkled his nose and hurried past the gift shop and the administrator's office to the skilled nursing wing. He stood outside a room with 'Leon Smears' printed in black marker in a slide-in name holder on the wall beside the door. Norm removed the temporary card and slipped it into his pocket. *You won't need this much longer.*

He stepped inside and looked around the cramped quarters. He opened the narrow closet where a flannel robe, a birthday gift from Carin, hung alone on a wire hanger. He placed his briefcase inside and closed the door. The room felt cool and damp, like a crypt.

His father lay motionless except for the old man's eyes that had been following his son since he entered the room. Drool pooled in the corner of his mouth.

With his thumb and forefinger, Norm plucked off the blanket from the vinyl chair next to his father's bed. He frowned and held it at arm's length, dropping it in a heap in the corner next to the window where a spindly philodendron with brown-edged leaves drooped on the sill. Beside it sat a single card with a picture of an elephant in a party hat riding a tricycle and a caption that read, *Don't let them tell you it can't be done.* Inside, in spidery handwriting, the words *Get well soon* slanted above two signatures of the old man's only friends on earth.

"Hello, Leon." Norm tucked his coat under him as he sat on the edge of the chair. He undid a single button at the neck revealing brown and red plaid lining. "What have you been up to since I saw you last month? Still flirting with the nurses?" He forced a half-grin.

Norm leaned forward and squeezed his clasped hands between his knees. "How's the food in this joint?" He sank back in the chair, watching his father's face for some sign of recognition. "Oh, sorry, I forgot." He lifted the blanket that covered the skeletal frame with the toe of his loafer to reveal a six-inch tube, the diameter of a pencil, inserted into the old man's abdomen. When ALS, commonly known as Lou Gehrig's disease, paralyzed his father's throat along with the rest of his body, the nursing home inserted the feeding tube in accordance with the elder Smear's Advance Care Directive. When the doctor explained ALS and what they could expect, he told Norm that despite the physical ravages of the disease, ALS patients could retain their cognitive function until the end. He had reassured Norm that his father could understand everything said to him and even though he could only blink his replies—one for 'yes' and two blinks for 'no'—

they could still converse albeit in a mostly one-sided way.

That was fine with Norm.

"Bengals lost."

His father stared at his son through chalky pools of cataracts that clouded his vision.

"That's right, I forgot. Football isn't your game, is it? Now, the horses—that you get excited about. Every afternoon at the track, remember, Leon? And you'd give me twenty lousy bucks every Saturday for taking care of mom, the yard, house—all the stuff every teenage kid wants to be doing every goddamn day after school. I had no friends, couldn't play any sports because I had to be—your words—the *man of the house*—while you spent all your time and money—including *borrowing* back the twenties you gave me on Saturdays—on bad bets and boozing it up at River Downs."

His father blinked twice.

"No? Don't fuck with me, old man," Norm roared. He stood up and bent his face close to his father's. A tear from his eye landed on the papery skin of the old man's cheek. "And even when you came to the hospital when mom was dying, you were so drunk you couldn't even say, 'Goodbye'. Remember that, *Dad?* And you wondered why I changed my name? Because I set my sights on bigger dreams than a bottle of Jack and a hundred buck win at the track. So I took Seitz, mom's name before you ruined her life."

Norm straightened up and breathed heavily. He walked over to the window where he watched visitors and staff entering and exiting the building. He buttoned his coat and turned around. "I didn't come to fight with you. I just came by to pay the rent on this dump." He scowled at his father and laughed mirthlessly as he looked around at the faded green paint on the walls and worn floor tiles. He retrieved his briefcase and set it on the foot of the bed. He opened the case and ran his fingers along the Ruger's grip for a full minute without looking up before he spoke. "Will you do me one last favor?"

The icy blue eyes watered back.

"Die before I have to cough up next month's eight grand."

SIXTEEN

Velma Gates turned down the sound on the television. She had already seen every episode of *Real Housewives of New Jersey* but she never tired of the catfights. Watching the show always made her feel better about her own family—*warts and all* as GG liked to say.

She strained to hear what Big Roy and Norm were talking about in the kitchen. She caught a couple of phrases, *CLAW and Schwab*, but that was all. She kicked off the afghan while she cursed at the massive dog that refused to budge from where he slept at the foot of the sofa. "Move yourself, Moose, you damn flea motel." She pushed the mongrel onto the floor while she searched under the blanket for her slippers.

Big Roy sipped on a glass of iced, caramel-colored liquid. A bottle of Jim Beam sat beside a 2-liter of Pepsi in the center of the table.

"Did ya offer our guest a drink?" Velma asked her husband as she shuffled across the room.

The men watched Velma check out the contents of the refrigerator before turning her attention to the freezer. She rummaged around until she found what she was looking for.

"He's not staying. Besides, I got important business with another party."

"Oh yeah, I forgot. You're mister big-shot, mister hoity-toity." Velma pulled up a seat at the card table in the corner of the room where a new puzzle box waited for her. She plunked down the Cookie Dough ice cream and squeezed a generous helping of chocolate syrup into the carton. Velma shoveled a heaping spoonful of the sundae into her mouth, then dumped the box of puzzle pieces onto the table.

"You ever heard of a bowl, woman?" Big Roy added some whiskey to his glass.

"Like I said, Norman, Big Roy here has gone all highfalutin'. Too good for the likes of us."

Norm shuddered at the idea he had had anything in common with Velma, even if it was only a low opinion of Big Roy. When a stinkbug meandered across the table in front of him, Norm pulled the collar of his coat tight under his chin.

Big Roy brushed aside the bug. He pushed a manila folder across the table. "Like I told you, that's all I got. Them CLAWs are grabbing up everything in the county. Like it or not, the tree-huggers got a big pile of government money behind them and they're not shy about throwing it around."

"Yeah, I know. They've been bugging me..." He paused when he caught another stinkbug sluggishly making its way across the windowsill. "They keep calling me about Schwab's property. I got other plans, as you know." He watched Big Roy avoid eye contact by mixing himself another drink.

"You're still on board, aren't you? We have a gentleman's agreement..."

Hearing that, Velma snorted ice cream out her nose.

"Have you got something to say to me, old woman?" Big Roy rose from his seat. He balled his fists.

Norm decided he'd had enough for one day. He slipped the file folder into his briefcase. "I'll be in touch. Stop by the office when you aren't so busy." He snapped the clasp on his case shut. "If this pans out, I'll have some money for you."

"Oh, yeah, Norm. There's another item in there you might find interesting." Big Roy winked.

...

Norm sat in his car. Before he left, he wanted to check the latest property Big Roy had scouted for him. He opened the file. *Vacant at least four months. Owner whereabouts unknown. Decent neighborhood. I should be able to unload this pretty fast. Okay, Big, this will work. Let's see what else we've got.*

He read through the second document. It was a life insurance policy that Violet Schmidt sold back to Money Matters. If Violet died, he stood to make a big payoff. The senior center was proving to be a lucrative playing ground even if he did have to share the winnings with his finder. Norm sensed something was up with Roy and figured it was time to cut the old sod loose. As Bobo said, one bad apple spoiled the pie. That should be an analogy Big Roy would appreciate.

Norm placed the file in his briefcase and set it on the floor in back of his seat. *Fingers crossed, Vi."*

He was backing the car out when the van driven by Steve

Ober pulled up beside him. Harvey Johnson occupied the passenger seat.

This is interesting.

Steve waved at Norm and opened the door. Harvey came around to the driver's side of the vehicle. He motioned with his hand for Norm to open his window.

Norm put down the window. "Hello, boys. What brings the CLAWs out on a day like this?" He smiled at his own joke.

Harvey shrugged as he leaned against the door of the Hummer. "I could ask you the same thing. Aren't you worried about getting this beautiful vehicle all wet?" Harvey looked up at the dark sky. He held out his palm.

"I'm more concerned that some yokel might think it's okay to rub his grimy jacket against my brand new wax job." Norm stared down the other man. "I'd have to say, that might make me forget my sunny disposition, who knows?"

"Speaking of sunny dispositions," Steve interjected, "how's Carin?"

Norm pursed his lips. With one finger, he wiped nonexistent dust off the dashboard. "She's having a hard time." He looked from Steve to Harvey, his eyes like molten lead. "It doesn't help that you two are after her like buzzards tracking a field mouse for your chance to grab Schwab's land," his voice rose. "So consider yourselves warned, CLAWs, back off." He threw the car into reverse and spun around spitting gravel in his wake.

SEVENTEEN

Hank turned to the local news section of *The Goose Down Daily News*. "Let me bring you up to date." He scanned the page. "Here we go, *Letters to the Editor*. That's always fun."

The whoosh of the respirator pumping life-sustaining air into Tippi's lungs was the only response.

"Here's a good one: *Dear Editor, I am writing to you as a last resort. This town needs to do something about the millions of geese that have invaded our town and are leaving their mark(s), if you get my drift, all over the place. City council won't do a (bleeping) thing but told me I should check the sign with our city name on my way out of town. I am offering to shoot the nuisances —the geese, not the council (although that's not a terrible idea)— and rid our town of these disgusting, disease-carrying varmints (again, geese, not council). I am asking that you print a copy of the petition I will be circulating on Saturday giving me permission to do as stated above. I am looking for other concerned citizens for help in this matter. I can be reached at snarkygranny@gmail.com.*

"What do you think? Should I fire up the old twelve gauge and join the fight?" Hank folded the paper before he tossed it in the trash. He pulled his chair closer to Tippi's bed and massaged her hand.

"Can you hear me, Tabitha? Talk to me, baby." He stroked her forehead and tucked a loose pink curl behind her ear. "Bet you never thought you'd hear me say that, did you honey?" He thought he saw her eyes open if only for a second.

"Tippi?" Hank gripped her hand. "It's me, Hank. Squeeze my hand if you understand." Did he imagine it or was there a barely discernible response? "Hold on, honey, I'm going to get the nurse. Don't go anywhere," he joked, hoping to get a reaction.

Hank stood outside Tippi's room. The glass-fronted rooms in the ICU were arranged in a semi-circle around the nurses' station. Hank saw several nurses busy attending to other patients. Finally, one of the two male RNs finished up and was heading back to the station when Hank waved him over.

"Mr. Klaber. How's she doing today?" Herman asked.

Hank liked the young man who like himself had served in the Marines. The ICU was a busy place where lives hung in the balance but the nurse always answered Hank's questions honestly with a patience even Hank didn't feel he deserved.

Hank tried not to be a pest but this was the woman he loved more deeply than he ever thought possible. After the death of his wife of more than forty years, he'd resigned himself to living the rest of his life alone. His only family now was his adult daughter who lived in Cincinnati with her husband and Hank's only grandchild, Noah. These were the people he would step in front of a speeding train to protect.

Then, Tippi Mulgrew careened into his life on a senior trip to Paris when they shared a seat on the RC Racer at Euro Disney.

"Herman," Hank tried to contain his excitement, "I think she responded to me. She heard me, I know it."

Herman listened, expressionless.

"I was reading some dumb letter in the paper and she opened her eyes. It wasn't much, but I saw it. I know I did."

Herman placed a steady hand on Hank's shoulder. "Mr. Klaber, I…"

"Hank, please. Just Hank."

"Right." Herman nodded.

"I saw it—I know it wasn't much—but it was there. It was." Hank shifted from one foot to the other. He couldn't stand still, he was too excited. "And she squeezed my hand."

"You may be right," Herman said, his words calm, measured.

"Then she's coming around, she's getting better, right?"

"Hold on, Hank." He pressed Hank's shoulder. "I need you to hear me, okay?"

Hank nodded. His mind was on the still figure behind him and the glimmer of hope he couldn't—no, wouldn't—let slip away. He pretended to pay attention as Herman's steady voice slid over him like melting snow on a warm mitten—you want to hold on to it but nature—in Hank's case, human nature—had other ideas.

"The body is an amazing piece of technology," Herman was saying. He tried to appeal to Hank the engineer, the analyst. "Even in cases like Ms. Mulgrew's, a patient may exhibit reflex movements such as you describe that are in no way responses to what we say or even do—like squeezing someone's hand. It's like when you have a twitch. It's the involuntary movement of a muscle." Herman's phone went off but he wanted to offer Hank something to hold on to. "Keep doing exactly what you're doing. It's good medicine."

Good for him anyway, the nurse thought as he hurried to the next patient.

Hank's thoughts drifted to what he could say to make her let him know he was getting through? He started to go back inside the room when Mr. Wittekind and Elrod Klienfelter got off the elevator.

"Hank, it's us," Wittekind called in a stage whisper and waved across the floor.

Elrod elbowed his companion in the side. He put a finger to his lips.

Mr. Wittekind carried a spring bouquet of colorful flowers. Elrod held a red balloon with the words "Get Well" inscribed in gold letters across the front. Both men were dressed in dark suits accented by matching, paisley bow ties.

Hank waved at GG Gates who pushed a cart of cleaning supplies into a room across from Tippi's, vacated that morning when the patient went into cardiac arrest and died. Everything about the place was a reminder of the thin line between this life and the next.

As he waited for the two men to join him, he positioned himself sideways in the door to Tippi's room to prevent the two visitors from barging in. They weren't exactly known for being subtle.

"You guys look awfully spiffy," Hank said, shaking each man's hand. "Glad to see you back on your feet."

"It was like we were on a little vacation," Elrod said. "Great food, pretty nurses. We're better than ever."

Wittekind grinned broadly. "We got dates."

"We met some ladies..." Elrod said. He broke into a laugh so loud the group drew stern looks and shushes from a couple exiting the next room.

"Let's step over to the visitors' lounge." Hank pointed his chin to a family room down the hall. "You can tell me all about it."

Hank opened the door to the small room furnished with a lone plastic, orange love seat. An old television sat angled on a low table in the corner.

Elrod perched on the edge of the seat. He ran his fingers down the crease in his pants legs. Mr. Wittekind leaned against the wall. Elrod looked at him questioningly and patted the seat beside him.

Wittekind shook his head. "Don't want to wrinkle." He rubbed the toe of one shiny oxford against the back of his calf. "Gotta make a good first impression. This could be the one."

"When did all this happen?" Hank tried to seem interested.

"After we saw our lives pass before our eyes, we signed up for a dating site when we got out of the hospital," Wittekind said. "Life's short, you know."

"We went online," Elrod added.

"He knows it was online," Wittekind said. "You said 'site' so obviously..."

Hank was losing his composure. He wanted, no, *needed,* to get back to Tippi. "Tell me about your future brides." *God, give me patience—or a gun to shoot myself.*

"My lady's name is Pansy. She's divorced." Wittekind wiggled his eyebrows in Groucho Marx fashion.

"Mine's Rosemary," Elrod said. "They're twins." The men beamed at Hank. "We're taking them to Olive Garden."

"We're pulling out all the stops," Wittekind said.

"We tossed a coin, Golden Corral or Olive, and the Garden won," Elrod said. He looked worried. "I hope we're doing the right thing."

Hank fought a smile. He tried to match the men's concern over restaurant choices. "I think that's exactly the right place for a first date. Start out with a nice bottle of wine..."

"Wine?" Elrod twisted his hands and looked to Wittekind. "We don't know anything about wine. Now, beer we could handle. How about beer?"

"I think this calls for wine. You do want to the ladies to think you're two suave gentlemen, right?"

"Well, yeah," Wittekind said. "But how do we...?"

"Ask the waiter for a recommendation. He'll steer you right." Hank looked at his watch. He wanted to get back to Tippi. "Better say 'hi' to our girl before you go."

EIGHTEEN

Sheriff Grange stood with Amy, Zenobia and Moira in the fellowship hall of the Congregational Church. "Nice service."

"Let's sit down, Pete." Zenobia pointed to an empty table in the back. "I realize I'm spittin' in the wind but you need to pace yourself."

"That's what I told him." Amy took the sheriff's hand and led him to the table. The others followed and arranged themselves in a half-circle where they could watch the mourners line up to shake Norm's hand and hug Carin.

"Look at that guy," Moira said, scowling. "He acts like he's lord of the manor opening his castle to the peasants."

Amy nodded. "Wonder what will happen to the Schwab's farm? I heard CLAW had been talking with them about putting it into a land trust. Do you think Carin will go through with it?"

"That depends on whether Norm thinks he can make some money on the deal," Grange said. He got up and pushed back his chair. "Hold that thought." He spotted Hank in the doorway and crossed the room to meet him. He waited while his friend made his way through the receiving line to greet Carin.

"You doing okay, sweetie?" Hank put a fatherly hand on her

shoulder.

She sighed. "If I have to meet any more of *them,*" she whispered, directing her sights to a giant in an expensive-looking, black suit standing with Bobo Fowler next to Norm, "I might grab Sauerkraut, jump on the Harley and leave town."

"That guy could double as a sequoia in a horror film," Grange commented, stepping forward.

"Marion. He just stands there watching everybody. And, that little weasel, Bobo... Gives me the creeps," Carin shrugged. "It's been a long few days. I'm looking forward to getting out of these heels, putting on my pj's and climbing into bed for a week or two."

"You know if there's anything at all..." Hank said.

"I do." She squeezed his hand. She looked from Hank to the sheriff. "Thanks for coming, guys. It means a lot." She pasted on a smile and turned back to Norm and his growing circle of guests.

"Join us, Hank?" Grange pointed his chin at Amy who waved back.

"Sure." Hank followed the sheriff across the room. He nodded to some members from the center who sat clustered in groups, talking in low whispers.

"You look beat," Zenobia said as Hank shot a look of gratitude at Amy who motioned for him to sit. The coroner hesitated. She debated whether or not she should ask about Tippi. "I can get you some coffee and I think there are some sandwiches..."

"Thanks, but I can't look at another cup of coffee—or a sandwich. I've been hanging out in the hospital cafeteria between times with Tippi and I'm full up of coffee and turkey sandwiches."

"Tippi?" Amy asked.

"She's..." He cleared his throat and paused before he went on, "her condition is still critical."

"Keep talking to her. You might be surprised what she'll remember when she comes to," Zenobia said.

Hank brightened. "You know, I think she looked at me and squeezed my hand. I think she knew I was there."

"Uh oh." Moira nodded at Norm who headed in their direction. She leaned back in her chair and crossed her arms across her chest.

"How's it going, ladies and gents?" Norm smiled down. He pulled up a folding chair, turned it around and straddled it. He stretched out his long legs and rested his chin on his hands.

"How's Carin?" Zenobia asked by way of greeting.

"Oh, you know." Norm shrugged. His eyes wandered the room as he spoke.

"Looking for somebody?" Moira asked curtly.

He turned his attention back to the group. "Just trying to be a good host," he bristled. "Oh, and by the way, deputy, stay away from my vehicle."

"I have no idea what you're talking about." Moira stood up and slung her purse over her shoulder. "I think that's my cue to head back to the station. Catch the rest of you guys later."

"I don't think me and Deputy Potts got off on the right foot," Norm said, watching Moira wend her way through the tables and head for the door.

Hank pointed to Mr. Wittekind across the room. "And he's off." The older man ran a comb through what there was of his hair, picked up his cane and tottered out the door after Moira.

"That old coot won't let a little food poisoning keep him away from a pretty lady," Norm observed. "Gotta admire that." He sounded wistful.

"What? Bein' an old letch?" Amy asked.

"No." Norm paused a full minute before he spoke again. "His self-confidence. Seeing himself a certain way—even if nobody else does." He stared up at the fluorescent light fixture overhead where one of the long bulbs sputtered and blinked.

Hank pictured a nervous Wittekind dressed up in his black suit and bow tie hoping to meet 'the one'. "Yeah, maybe we got him all wrong."

Amy raised her eyebrows and glanced sideways at Grange. Zenobia ran a hand down her lime green sweater and buried her face in the pink, fur-trimmed collar.

"Guess you got your hands full with all the extra work at Ernie's?" Grange asked, breaking the tension.

Norm offered a half-smile. "I got Little Roy and Baby looking after the livestock. Lucky for me those two have nothing better to do."

"You actually gave those losers permission to...?" Grange's mouth dropped.

"It's not like I gave them keys for chrissakes. Old man Schwab did that when he bought the place. Gave 'em keys to the shed, the guesthouse and Schwab had keys to Roy's. People around here do that, especially the ones separated from their neighbors the way these guys are. That's what Little Roy told me when I offered to get a set made for him. I guess if they wanted anything, it's gone by now."

The sheriff shook his finger at Norm. "Get their keys back though by now they've contaminated the entire place. This whole mess just keeps getting worse. BCI is going out there tomorrow. I'm going to lose my badge over this." He looked to Amy for support.

Zenobia patted Grange's shoulder. "You want something to disappear, just let those Gates' have a crack at it."

The others nodded.

"I'd hate to be the one to clean up after *that* outfit," Grange said. "They got a couple dozen old cars, or parts I should say, scattered all over their farm. I got after Big Roy once about a pile of old tires he had down by the creek and the next day I get a call there's a fire at their place. Turns out he tried to burn 'em up and the damn things smoldered for three days. Whole neighborhood stank for weeks."

"His father would have a fit if he could how Big Roy let the place to go," Zenobia said. "I remember when we were kids how the old man would look the other way when we climbed his fence and stole apples from his orchard. I broke my arm once when I'd climbed up one of his trees. I was tossing fruit to some kid, I can't remember his name, when I lost my balance and down I went." She smiled, remembering. "Spent the rest of the summer in a cast—plaster in those days. But you know what old man Gates did?" She looked around the table. "He sent my mother an entire bushel of apples, 'for the baby' he said."

"Doesn't sound like he passed any of those qualities on to his son," Amy said.

Zenobia shook her head, agreeing. "No." She fished in her

purse and retrieved a pack of nicotine gum. She wrinkled her nose and popped a stick in her mouth before she continued her story. "Of course, my mother was so mad at me for stealing, she wouldn't let me have a single apple. She said Mr. Gates supported his family by selling those apples and what I did was taking the food right out of his kids' mouths. Believe me, I never stepped foot over there again."

"You were just a kid," Norm said. He felt in his pants pocket and pulled out a pink jar with a gold lid. He made sure he had the attention of everyone at the table before he removed the lid and applied a generous amount of the contents to his lips. "Great stuff. I get it specially made for me by a Chinese herbalist in Philadelphia."

"Can I try it?" Amy asked. She reached across the table.

"Sorry, sweetheart. Not at these prices." Norm screwed on the lid and returned the jar to his pants pocket. "Anyway," he turned his attention to the sheriff, avoiding Amy's scowl. "I told the boys they could hunt or target practice on the place if they'd make sure the animals were fed and watered and if they did that, I'd throw in a couple of Ernie's old shotguns and some ammo he had stockpiled. I have to get rid of all that stuff anyway. Clearing out the barn alone is going to take months."

"Now I'm going to have to go and tell 'em to stay out. Great. Maybe losing my badge wouldn't be the worst that could happen to me. Flippin' burgers at the *Castle* sounds good. All the free sliders I could eat."

Amy held her nose and shook her head.

Norm stood up. "I get it, sheriff. I hope it won't take too long. I have plans for the property and some of my *associates* don't like to be kept waiting." He watched his wife return a hug from Dr. Schneider who had just arrived. "I better get back to Carin. See you people later."

Across the room, Dr. Schneider shook Norm's hand and spoke briefly to the couple. Norm pointed out the sheriff's table and the doctor made his way to join them, stopping to say a few words at the other tables along the way.

"Folks," Dr. Schneider greeted them. His exhaustion showed in his stooped shoulders and the dark circles under his eyes.

"Good afternoon, Doc. Pull up a seat." Zenobia scooted her chair over to make room next to her.

"They just set out a new tray of snacks. I'm going to nab it before anybody else does." Amy patted Dr. Schneider's shoulder and hurried to the food table one step ahead of Elrod.

"Sorry, this one's mine," she told him and hurried back to her table with the tray. One of the caterers followed her with plates, cups and a fresh pot of coffee.

No one spoke as the food was passed and the drinks poured. "I needed that," Dr. Schneider said after washing down a bite of his ham and cheese sandwich with a long drink of black coffee.

"Rough morning?" Zenobia asked.

He looked ashen when he answered, "You could say that."

The others glanced at each other and waited.

"I have more bad news." He spoke slowly, his voice low.

Hank started to rise but the doctor shook his head and waved his hand for him to sit.

"No, Hank. Tippi's condition is unchanged." He cleared his

throat. "Violet Schmidt died a few hours ago."

NINETEEN

Sheriff Grange stood beside Amy at Tippi's bedside. Between the two of them they finally persuaded Hank to take a much-needed afternoon off by offering to fill in for a few hours. Only after Hank had written his cell phone number in large, red letters on the whiteboard by the door and made Amy promise to call immediately if there was any change in Tippi's condition—good or bad—did he agree to go.

"I'm going, but only to run by the house for a quick shower and to change clothes." Hank kept one hand clasped on the doorframe, his eyes on Tippi.

"And," Amy said, prying open his fingers, "I've made you an appointment for a massage at Flights of Fancy and called the diner to expect you for dinner." If he failed to show for either of these appointments, Amy warned, he would answer to her and that was not something either of them wanted.

Grange said he'd learned the hard way not to cross this woman who in spite of her petite size and big blue eyes, could make a grown man weep. "And not metaphorically," Grange told Hank. "For real. I saw her do it."

With a parting kiss on Tippi's forehead, Hank left.

"I need to take this," Grange said when a call came in on his cell. "I'll be right back."

The sheriff stepped into the corridor. The call was brief and when he re-entered the room and faced Amy, his shoulders slumped. "Arsenic." He sat down on the side of the bed.

Amy took his hand and together they watched the rhythmic rise and fall of Tippi's breathing as the ventilator did its work.

Amy broke the silence. "How?"

"Hazelnut flavored coffee. Still testing other possible sources but so far everything else came back clean." He sat quietly watching the rise and fall of Tippi's chest as the ventilator did its work.

"Oh, my God." She stared at him in disbelief.

Grange shook his head. "We'll check the well water on Ernie's land but Ernie's death was attributed to the flu so there was no reason to suspect foul play. And," he hesitated, "we know Gert took a lot of the leftovers from Ernie's wake, including the coffee, to the center for the mahjong tournament."

"Right after you went to talk with Victor was when you got sick too," Amy reminded him. "You said Arcella gave you coffee and..."

He grimaced. "Believe me, I haven't forgotten." He took Amy's hand. This mess just got a whole lot messier."

Amy kissed his cheek. "Is there anything I can do to help?"

"Just being here..." Grange coughed into his hand. "I need to high-tail it over to Schwab's place."

He stood up and picked up his hat from Tippi's tray table. "I could be in hot water over this one since all of the Rays had access to the place. Damn." He punched the crown of his hat and slammed it on his head.

"You do know you're not really Superman, don't you?" Amy adjusted the hat and straightened his tie.

Grange looked down at this tiny person. He towered over her, he carried a gun and he was Goose Down's top law enforcement officer, but he wondered which of the two of them was the scariest. He didn't want to admit it, but he was pretty sure he knew.

"Can you find a ride home? I don't know when I'll be done."

Amy wrapped her arms around the sheriff. "Don't worry about me, I'll be fine." She stepped back and looked at the face of the man she had grown to know so well in a few short months. She smoothed his collar and brushed his cheek with her lips. "You're a good man, Peter Grange. I love you."

...

Norman followed his wife into Tippi's room. He waved at Amy and took a seat on the foot of the bed while continuing a heated conversation on his cell phone. "I gotta go. I'm visiting a friend in the hospital." He paused, then added, "I'll get back to you. Don't do anything stupid. In fact, don't do anything at all until you hear from me." He clicked off and smiled at Carin and Amy. "And they say a woman's work is never done."

Carin and Amy exchanged glances. Amy raised her eyebrows.

"Has there been any improvement?" Carin asked.

Amy rose and motioned for Carin to take her seat. "No. Hank thought she opened her eyes and squeezed his hand but I haven't seen anything like that since I've been here. She sighed and looked down at the still figure. "Hank brought in her Kindle and I've been reading from it. Did you know Tippi's a big fan of Romance novels?"

"I had no idea," Carin said. She looked across the bed at Norm.

He answered with a shrug and dialed another number on his phone. He walked around to the other side of the bed and spoke in a low voice. He turned his back to the women and put his free hand up to cover the side of his face.

"I've been reading *Fifty Shades of Grey* to her," Amy said with a blush. "She's got the entire trilogy." She showed Carin the book list on Tippi's e-reader. "I figured if anything could get a reaction, Christian Grey would be the man for the job."

Carin's red curls bounced above her shoulders when she laughed. "Finally, I've got something to hold over her. I'm never going to let her live this down." Carin gasped and covered her mouth when she realized what she'd said.

"It's okay." Amy patted her shoulder. "Here," she said handing Carin the Kindle, "why don't you take over for a while. She'd probably enjoy hearing a fresh voice. And," she pointed to the page, "I need to try and shake these images out of my brain."

The sheet around Tippi's feet rustled, startling the women. "Did you do that?" Carin asked her husband.

"Huh?" Norm placed his hand over the phone. "Do what?"

"Nothing, I guess. Just imagining things."

Norm resumed speaking in a low voice. "Right, Violet Schmidt. I can come to your office to pick it up." He listened. "How long to process? Are you effing kidding me?" He rolled his eyes. "I guess I don't have a choice, do I?" He punched 'off'.

"Do you think she can hear us?" Carin said. She leaned in and stroked Tippi's forehead. "Can you hear me? It's Carin. I understand you're a fan of steamy novels."

Tippi's breathing paused.

"So, you like Christian Grey, do you?" Amy said.

No reaction.

"Wait until I tell your fans down at Gaggle of Giggles that their favorite performer is a sucker for romance stories—*Fifty Shades* to be exact. That will get a bigger laugh than any of your stand-up routines ever did," Carin goaded.

The women searched their friend's face for a reaction. "Am I seeing it because I want to so badly, or did she open her eyes for a minute?" Carin rubbed Tippi's cheek hoping for a response. "There," she said and prodded her again, "see that? She opened her eyes." Carin aimed her finger again but was stopped when Amy caught her friend's hand before it reached its mark.

"The nurse said these are just reflex actions. They don't mean anything." Amy saw the same disappointed look on Carin's face she'd seen on Hank's when the doctor went over this point with him again.

Amy's cell phone rang. She smiled and shook her head when she answered. "Hello, Hank." She offered some reassuring words. "Carin and Norm are here. We've got it covered, so enjoy your pie and we'll see you in a while."

"Have you had your dinner?" Carin said when Amy hung up.

"No, I'm not really hungry," she looked over at Tippi, "but I could use the opportunity to get some fresh air and I'd like to stretch my legs a bit.

...

Carin looked up from the Kindle. She rubbed the back of her neck. "I can't take any more of Christian and Anastasia and their ridiculous antics. I feel like I need to take a shower with disinfectant."

Norm stopped his pacing and turned to his wife. "Anything in there we could use? Spice things up a bit?""

Carin ignored the comment.

"Want me to take over?"

"Would you? That would be great." Before he could change his mind, she made a beeline for the door. "I have an errand to run." She waved and called over her shoulder, "Back later."

Norm took the seat his wife vacated and pulled up the page she'd just read. He scrolled ahead and frowned. "Damn, Tippi. I can't read this crap out loud." He powered off the device and set it aside.

"Let's see. What else would you like to talk about? The weather? Pretty nice. Politics? Pretty shitty. ISIS, global warming, global cooling?" He watched the steady in and out of her breathing. He checked his phone.

"You think you got problems? Let me tell you something. Yours are nothing compared to the shit-load of trouble I'm in." He stood and went to look out the window where he spotted Carin's car waiting at the intersection.

"I'm drowning, Tippi. Debt up to—no, over—my ears. I've broken so many laws—legal, moral, you name it, and I've done it. And you know what?" He glanced at the briefcase he'd set in the corner. "There's only one way out and I'm too much of a coward to take it." He turned his gaze back outside.

"And that woman," he pointed to Carin pulling into traffic, "she's going to go right down the tubes with me." He choked. "But, she did refuse to sign for a second mortgage on the house," his voice became angry, "She wouldn't have signed off on it herself so I had to. What else could I have done? I'm desperate. I owe everybody; my old man's nursing home, those worthless pieces of paper from F.U. that set me back forty grand, not to mention what I was already in to Bobo for..." His laugh was bitter. "And you want to hear something funny, Tippi? I tried to convince myself I was doing this for her—for us." He went and stood at the foot of the bed. He gazed down at the still figure and played with the diamond-studded ring on his pinky finger. "At least Violet bought me..."

His cell phone rang. "Sorry, I have to take this." He swiped the screen and answered, "Seitz." He glanced down at Tippi and walked to the doorway while keeping an eye on the still figure.

He listened to the caller, his breathing growing more and more shallow. "Yeah, Roy, I'm still here." He listened then punched 'Off' and threw the phone across the room where it landed at the foot of the bed. He ran a hand through his hair and went to the window.

"Well, do you want to hear the latest?" he said. "It's that damn Big Roy. He must have closed the deal with CLAW right after I left his place." He turned to Tippi. "Can you believe it? The idiot. We were set to make five times what those damn tree huggers offered. A couple of hundred grand—peanuts. Roy claims he couldn't give up the farm. Too many memories. That's bull. This way, he keeps the property and gets the money. Maybe he's not as dumb as he looks, after all."

Norm sank into the chair beside the bed. "Our deal was to combine Ernie and Gates' properties for development. A golf course, condos. With Fowler and his investors backing the plan, Bobo said we'd be millionaires several times over." He threw back his head and let go something between a sob and a laugh. "No honor among thieves, right?"

He stood up. He jammed his hands in his pockets and began pacing around the bed. When he stopped, he said, "I'm gonna kill Gates—and Bobo's gonna kill me." He bent down and placed his lips close to her ear. "Unless I get him first," he whispered.

"Excuse me?" Tippi's nurse poked his head in the door. "I'm going to have to ask you to let me have Ms. Mulgrew for a bit. Doctor's ordered a CT scan so she'll be a while. Mr. Klaber just arrived and is in the family lounge if you'd like to join him."

Norm wearily gathered up his coat and turned to Tippi. "Thanks for listening." He started to leave then turned back and took her hand. 'I hope you make it, Tippi. You're a good woman and I miss you—even when you give me the business in your act down at *Giggles.*"

"See you later."

The room was quiet except for the beeping of monitors and whoosh of the air pump. Tippi Mulgrew lay still in her own silent world.

A young woman in burgundy scrubs hurried into the room. She disconnected wires and monitors and unlocked the wheels on Tippi's bed. Lastly, she checked her patient's armband against the screen on her iPad. "We're good to go. Ready, sweetie?"

The last word was no sooner spoken than Tabitha Mulgrew's hand shot out from beneath the blanket and grasped the aide's hand in a grip so powerful, the woman yelped in pain.

"What the?"

Tippi opened her eyes.

TWENTY

"It's okay, Victor." Grange motioned for him to sit. "Did Deputy Potts explain why you're here?"

Victor nodded. He placed his clasped hands on the table and leaned forward. His voice shook when he said, "Sheriff, have you seen Arcella? Is she okay? I need to be with her. Please."

The sheriff sat down across from him. Moira turned her chair so she could see both men easily.

"She's right next door, Victor." Grange nodded at his deputy. The red light of a camera blinked in the corner.

...

Sheriff Grange propelled his way through the gauntlet of reporters crowding the small lobby of the Goose Down courthouse. The case had drawn widespread attention and correspondents from the major networks were represented. Grange knocked once at the prosecutor's office and shouldered his way inside. He slumped against the door and stopped to catch his breath.

"Sheriff." The young prosecuting attorney poked his head above his cubicle wall. "What can I do for you?" He came out and offered Grange his hand.

"Just wondered if you have any idea how much time before my

case goes to trial?"

"That's up to the court but considering the criminal docket in Goose Down is pretty light," he cracked a half-smile, "my guess is less than six weeks."

"Do you know who caught the case?"

"Somebody so new she's still got a shine on her briefcase. She's in there now."

"Hoping to plea to manslaughter, I guess?"

The younger man nodded. "I'm sure."

"At least here, Victor and Arcella are away from those jackals." Grange inclined his chin to the door where a mob of reporters waited.

"Until they make bail anyway. Carin is working on that."

Grange frowned. "I can't believe they're involved. I know them. They're decent, hard-working folks."

"And you and I both know, Pete, people kill for a lot less than a couple acres of dirt."

...

Carin Seitz had decided to drive Gert's blue CRV hoping to avoid attracting attention. She kept the engine idling while she watched the courthouse across the street. Constructed near the end of the nineteenth century and designed in the Italianate style popular in mid-western towns of the time, the building consumed an entire city block. On this bright afternoon, reporters crowded onto the sweeping front staircase and wide, covered porch; some leaned against the Ionic columns, talking, smoking—oblivious to the man who limped out the side and melted into the lunch crowd of government staffers.

Seeing her target emerge, Carin threw the vehicle into drive and pulled the car into traffic. She saw her break, made a U-turn in the busy intersection, and pulled up alongside the sheriff. "Need a ride, sailor?"

Grange looked over his shoulder at the reporters, who spotted their quarry getting away, and ran toward him. He slid into the passenger's seat just before Carin peeled off into traffic. She barely missed an identical blue CRV behind her, prompting a middle finger salute from the white-haired driver.

"I ought to give you a ticket." Grange tightened his seatbelt.

His driver tapped the brake pedal. "Do you want me to let you out?"

He shook his head. He checked the side mirror and watched the mob of reporters recede into the distance.

"Where'd you park?"

"The city lot." Grange's knuckles whitened as he gripped the panic handle above the door.

"We better not go back there yet. Probably be ambushed. How about we grab coffee somewhere quiet and I'll bring you back after? I have to make a quick stop at the hospital anyway before I go home. I have an early morning appointment at the bank about the bail and I have to get my paperwork together."

"Okay, but I'm going to need pie too." Grange's stomach growled.

Carin looked grim. "And, while you're wiping meringue off your nose, you can tell me why the hell you arrested Victor and Arcella."

TWENTY-ONE

Hank ran down the hall. He'd been at the drinking fountain when he noticed some unusual activity erupt around Tippi's room.

Please God...

He was stopped at the door by the nurses and aides clustered around her bed. One of the hospital doctors bent over her, intent on the sounds he heard in his stethoscope.

Carin came up behind Hank, her hand on his shoulder. "I just got back. What's going on?" she whispered in his ear.

He shook his head. "Can't tell."

A nurse spoke on her phone as she brushed past them on her way to another call.

Hank stepped in front of her. "What is it? What happened?"

She held the phone to her chest. "Doctor will be with you shortly," she said, hurrying on.

The group around Tippi began to break up and filter out. The doctor stood at the foot of the bed blocking Hank and Carin's view. He spoke again with a nurse before approaching the pair waiting outside.

The doctor smiled broadly and held out his hand to Carin, then to Hank. "You're the family?"

"Fiancé," Hank said. "And friend," he added.

"Well, we've got good news. But..." the doctor raised his palm before Hank could interrupt. "But, she's not yet out of the woods."

"Doc, give us the good news first." Hank grew impatient.

"She regained consciousness for about five minutes and responded appropriately to commands. Sometimes these things happen spontaneously and sometimes it's a trigger—kind of like an electric shock—that jolts the subconscious awake. The brain still holds a lot of mystery for medical science."

Hank shifted from foot to foot while the doctor spoke; his eyes searching for a sign of recognition from the still figure on the bed. "Thanks, doc, I'll go on in now and ..."

"Hold on." The doctor laid a restraining hand on Hank's arm. "That's only half of what I have to tell you."

Hank shook him off. "Well, get on with it, man."

"Hank," Carin said. "Let him finish."

The doctor flashed a smile at Carin. "Sometimes these remissions are only temporary, like the electric jolt analogy. We can only wait and watch and you should keep doing what you've been doing and if there's a particular word or phrase that gets even the slightest reaction, make a note on the whiteboard where the staff can see." His phone beeped. "Gotta go." He started to hurry away then turned back. "I told you she responded to commands. When I asked her the year and who the president is, she answered right off. When she shaved ten years off her birth date, I knew for sure she understood me." He chuckled. "Works every time. But," he said, "maybe you can explain why she grabbed me by the collar—heck of a grip, by the way—why she said, and I quote, "'You tell your people that nobody, and I mean NOBODY, calls Tippi Mulgrew *sweetie.*'" The doctor rubbed his neck. "Any idea what she meant?"

. . .

Carin was seated in the cafeteria by the window overlooking the garden when Norm came up.

"Any news?"

Carin, her mouth full, held up a finger.

"Glad to see you haven't lost your appetite," Norm kidded his wife.

"Hold on." Carin washed down her food with a drink of water. She patted her mouth and leaned back in her seat. "Some good news for a change." She paused until she was sure she had her husband's full attention. "Tippi woke up."

Norm paled and leaned forward. "She…she woke up?"

Carin forked salad into her mouth and nodded.

"Did she say anything? How do you know she was really awake? I mean, maybe…"

"No. The doctor said she responded to his commands appropriately. She woke up, alright."

"Is she…is she awake now?"

"Unh uh. The doctor said it was probably something she heard that jolted her brain and caused her to come to. Then she was out again."

"Shit," Norm blurted out. He grimaced when he realized what he'd said. "I'm just sorry that she—you know," he explained seeing his wife's shock at his reaction. He rubbed his temples.

"Hmm," Carin frowned. "What'd you say to her? Some big

secret like you're having a torrid love affair with Velma Gates?" She tried to lighten the mood.

"Right. "Now you know."

"Hank is with her now," Carin went on. "The doctor said we should keep talking to her and see if anything we say could be a trigger that could bring her around. I think once she wakes up and starts talking, all sorts of stuff we've been telling her will come out. Should be pretty funny."

"Yeah. A real riot."

Carin looked hard at her husband. "You don't seem too happy about this. What's going on?"

"No, no. I am. I just had some other disturbing news earlier."

"I'm sorry." Carin reached over and took her husband's hands in hers. "Want to talk about it?"

He sighed. "It's that damn Gates."

"Big Roy?"

"Yeah. He called to tell me he sold one of those easements on his property to CLAW. The dumbass sold out for a fraction of what he could've made with me." He made a slicing motion across his throat when a cafeteria worker stopped to wipe off the adjoining table. When she'd gone, he went on, "He and I had a deal. I've got developers ready to invest but only on the combined properties."

"Combined?"

"Gates' and Ernie's of course. What do you think?" He leaned across the table, his face the color of the cherry tomato in his wife's salad.

"What I think is that *I* will decide what will happen to my father's property—now *my* property—and that will be to abide by dad's wishes to put it all into a land trust, minus the five acres I'm gifting to the Alvarezes."

Norm half-rose from his seat and pounded the table with his fist. "You mean those damn Mexicans who poisoned your own parents? You're as stupid as…" He shook his fist at her. "You live in the ivory tower I—that's I—built for you and you don't have a damn clue…" He pushed over his chair and stormed off.

Carin's face turned white. Norm had never raised his voice to her before and certainly never threatened her with physical harm. Something was terribly wrong and she had no idea what it was.

TWENTY-TWO

Velma Gates chewed her lip. She glanced at her husband who studied the contents of the file folder in front of him. She tapped her polished red nails on the gleaming surface of the long table in the conference room at Ripcoff, Ripcoff and Ripcoff, Attorneys at Law. "What did Norm say when you told him you was takin' CLAW's deal?"

"What could he say?" Big Roy said without looking up from the book he was reading. "If he's too dumb to pass on a sure thing, I guess that's his business. No art in no deal." Big Roy's shoulders shook with wet, wheezy guffaws. He wiped spittle off his chin with the back of his hand.

"What about the other work you do for 'im? You think he'll cut you outta it?"

"No. He can't afford to. I know where he's buried all the bodies. Hard to keep your fancy cars and high falutin' lifestyle much less be a big shot township trustee if you're in a jail cell."

That made Velma laugh so hard she swallowed her gum. "That's rich, Big."

The door opened and an elderly man in a wrinkled brown suit stepped inside. He was short—even by Velma's standards—and his thinning hair, the color of black shoe-polish, fringed above a high forehead and curled over the back of his frayed collar. His purple tie was decorated with a child's colorful handprints in what looked like finger-paints and hung down to his crotch. He took a seat at the head of the table and observed his clients.

"Afternoon, Ripcoff," Rig Roy greeted him. "Did you get my check?"

The lawyer nodded. "Shoulda charged you three times as much for that job. Next time you send me a client, get me one that can talk." He blinked in rapid succession. "Did you get that?"

Velma looked at her husband, her forehead wrinkled. "What's he mean, Big?"

Big Roy was saved from answering as the voices of Stephen Ober and Harvey Johnson entering the building drifted down the hall. The CLAWs, as Big Roy called them, chatted as the receptionist escorted the late arrivals into the room.

"Looks like we're the last ones at the party," Stephen joked, surveying the room's other occupants. He held out a hand to the elderly gentleman.

The older man ignored the hand and shook his head.

Stephen looked amused and moved to take a place across the table from Velma. He placed a camera on the table beside his briefcase and hung his jacket on the back of his chair. Harvey took a seat next to Stephen's.

"Will you do the introductions, Steve?" Harvey said.

Stephen opened his briefcase and brought out a sheaf of papers tabbed with varying colors to mark the sections. "Of course."

"Our donors, Mr. and Mrs. Gates," he said, smiling at the couple across from him. "Mr. Ripcoff, At...."

"Esquire," the old man croaked.

"Right," Stephen stuttered. "Mr. Ripcoff, Esquire," he added, smiling at the old man. "Attorney at Law. And I believe you all know Harvey Johnson and myself who are here to sign for C_AW."

"Get on with it," Ripcoff said.

"Of course," Stephen said and turned to the first tabbed page in his stack. "This states that our donors, Royal and," he hesitated and did a double take on the name. "Royal? Is that right?"

"Yeah," Big Roy said. "What about it?" His voice rose.

"Nothing. Nothing, at all. Just want to make sure we have it all right. Legal stuff, you know?" He looked at the attorney who was studying his tie. "Right, Mr. Ripcoff?"

"Huh?" The lawyer looked up, confused.

Harvey leaned back in his chair and closed his eyes.

"We done?" the lawyer asked.

"Soon as we all sign off and, of course, present Mr. And Mrs. Gates with their check for four-hundred and eighty-two thousand dollars." Stephen smiled at the Gates'. He explained that by signing the contract, the Gates were promising that their property would remain farmland in perpetuity and would not be sub-divided or developed. "To ensure compliance with today's agreement, CLAW retains the right to monitor the property once a year or more if there is evidence that the terms have been violated."

A soft snore emanated from the head of the table.

"That's our cue," Harvey said.

"Don't forget—we need a picture," Stephen said.

TWENTY-THREE

Sheriff Grange pushed his bifocals onto the top of his head. He rubbed the bridge of his nose and re-read the report in front of him. "Damn."

"Sheriff?" Moira called through the door.

"Come on in." Grange resettled his glasses and looked up at his deputy. "How's it going?" He motioned for her to take a seat.

"I'm going off shift and on my way to see Tippi. Thought I'd check with you first and see if there's anything you want me to do before I go?"

Grange snapped his fingers at the papers on his desk. "Not unless you can find some evidence in this report from the State Police that would clear the Alvarezes." He shook his head and scanned the report again. "The well on the place came back clean. He heaved a deep sigh. "As it stands, I would probably have to vote 'guilty' if I were on that jury."

"I just don't believe it," Moira said. "Besides being the sweetest two people in the world, what would be their motive? They'd be jeopardizing everything they worked so hard for—and risked their lives for, citizenship, a home of their own. It makes no sense."

"I agree, Moira. The problem is, I read this report a hundred times and the evidence points to them. Traces of old pesticide containing inorganic forms of arsenic—so deadly today it's banned in this country—were found on mud samples from the tires on the ATV Victor used to get around the property, and on his boots. And..." Grange raised his hand at his deputy who was about to interrupt, "and, ten thousand dollars in cash was found in Arcella's dresser drawer."

"But sheriff, that doesn't prove..."

"Deputy, traces of arsenic found in the bag of coffee in the Alvarezes pantry matched the one BCI tagged at the center the day of the poisonings. It also matches the residue in the travel mug I had with me the night I got sick. The lab is looking at the brownies as another possible source but those results haven't come back yet." He wiped his forehead and rested his head in his hand.

"But there were a lot of people in and out of the kitchen the day of the mahjong tournament. Anyone could have slipped the poison into that bag of coffee."

"That's true, but that doesn't explain the one at the Alvarez house. And, we haven't been able to come up with somebody else who might have a motive. Victor admitted he and Ernie had a big fight when he asked to buy five acres from Schwab to build a house for himself and Arcella. Schwab refused. He told Victor the entire three hundred acres was going into a land trust and he had an appointment set up with CLAW for the following week to fill out the paperwork. Unfortunately, Ernie died leaving Gert responsible for carrying out her husband's wishes. And, we know how that ended."

Moira swung her purse over her shoulder. "I get it, sheriff. Means, motive and opportunity. Investigations one-o-one."

The sheriff busied himself straightening the sheaf of papers and returned them to the file folder. "That's my cue to call it a day, deputy." He rose and opened the door. "After you. " He followed her into the hall.

...

Grange stopped at the front desk to inform Ed he was leaving for the day. He pictured Amy waiting for him at home while he waited for the officer to finish his phone call. It gave him a warm feeling to know he wasn't going back to an empty house and a frozen dinner washed down with the one beer he'd allowed himself every night after Ivy died. His stomach growled and he realized it had been hours since he'd eaten. *Pot roast, those little potatoes and that brown gravy I like. Maybe pie.* He ran a finger under the tight waistband of his uniform pants. He unbuttoned his trousers.

The desk sergeant hung up the phone, made some notes in the computer and looked up. "Takin' off, boss?"

"Yeah. I'm hoping a home-cooked meal and a good night's sleep will give me a new perspective on the case." He put on his hat. "So, if you have nothing else...?"

"Go home, boss. Say 'hello' to Amy for me." Ed turned his attention to an incoming phone call. "Hang on," he told the caller, placing a palm over the receiver.

Grange paused at the door and raised his eyebrows. "Yeah?"

The older man pointed at the sheriff's unbuttoned pants and grinned. "Might want to think twice about having seconds, boss."

He chuckled and turned his attention back to the business at hand.

TWENTY-FOUR

Norman Seitz parked his Hummer in the 'Fire Lane' in front of Fowler Tower and placed his township trustee placard in the front window. He checked the contents of his briefcase; the Ruger was nestled beneath the file folders. Norm fingered the files for a moment before removing the gun then locking it in the glove compartment. He flipped through the contents of the briefcase and satisfied that everything was in order, he went inside.

Bobo Fowler had gone all out when he renovated the century old structure that now bore his name in giant letters that flashed gold and white neon above the entrance. The building originally housed a factory that made uniforms for parochial schoolchildren throughout the Midwest and when Bobo bought the place back in the sixties, the red brick monstrosity was destined for the wrecking ball. Back then, workers on their way to lunch at the Woolworth counter or mothers dragging crying children by the ear to Karl's Kuts, had to dodge chunks of gray mortar dropping from the facade like goose scat. The interior was worse; a single freight elevator was the only access to the wooden floors upstairs where rows of women once bent over sewing machines ten hours a day, six days a week.

Now, the lobby boasted a gleaming marble floor and a colorful Chihuly chandelier that complemented the modern artwork and sculptures tastefully placed throughout. The offices on the upper floors featured oversized windows, spacious, airy floor plans and echoed the gilded glitz of the entryway. Bobo Fowler had successfully covered up all remnants of the building's seedy past. His own past on the other hand, remained a subject of debate among the good citizens of Goose Down, Ohio.

Norm paused at the desk in the center of the room and signed his name on the ledger the Security Guard pushed at him. The guard checked Norm's briefcase before he waved him through the metal detector. Once cleared, Norm stepped over to the elevator and pressed 'Up'.

...

Twenty minutes later, Norm was speeding back to his office. He was desperate to change out of the silk shirt that stuck to him like wallpaper paste. He pulled the damp shirtfront away from his chest only to feel it sucked back a moment later. He cranked up the vehicle's air conditioner even though the outside temperature was cooling in the advancing dusk of late afternoon. As he loosened his tie, he swerved towards the center of the road, managing to jerk the wheel back just in time to avoid a head-on collision with a Coca-Cola delivery truck. By the time he pulled into the parking place in front of his office, he was shivering with perspiration and cold, his face ashen.

Norm tried to wrap his brain around what had just happened. He'd been summoned to Fowler Tower where Bobo waited for him. Marion, the giant he'd met at Gert's funeral, sat in the corner hammering away at the keyboard of the laptop perched on his knee. He glanced up briefly when Norm came in before turning his attention back to the screen.

Even before the door closed behind him, Bobo began firing threats and accusations at Norm. *He hadn't even offered me a seat or a chance to explain; how I'd been screwed over by Big Roy Gates, recent events at the senior center that had turned the town upside down and real estate deals that were the last thing anybody wanted to think about. It's not my fault Bobo lives next door to Gates. Goodbye country club, swanky condos. Sorry, Bobo, guess you won't be waking up with a view of the ninth hole after all.*

Norm pulled down the car visor and checked his image in the mirror. *Seitz, you look like hell.* He ran a comb through his hair and straightened his tie. He put the Ruger back in his briefcase.

And what about Bobo's demand that he return his investment—with interest? Where was he supposed to get his hands on that kind if cash? Three hundred thousand? And counting?

What was that Bobo said? *Dead man walking?*

...

The office was deserted when Norm arrived and he welcomed the solitude while he figured out how to fix his problems with Bobo, with Carin and with the gigantic financial tsunami that was barreling toward him. He'd be damned if he'd go under without a fight.

Norm brought out the bottle of Macallan Single Malt Scotch he kept locked in his safe and poured three fingers into a tumbler. At three hundred dollars a bottle, he rarely indulged but tonight he needed an extra boost of confidence. He drank it quickly, poured another and slid into the Eames chair, his latest indulgence that Carin hadn't seen yet. He opened Spotify on his iPhone to an album of patriotic tunes by the Cincinnati Pops, leaned back into the buttery soft leather, sipped his whiskey and hummed along to the 1812 Overture. Finally, the tension began to ease from his body.

"Mr. Seitz? Are you in there?" The voice was followed by a loud pounding on the front door.

"Now what?" Norm leaped up. His phone followed the earphones still in his ears and swung precariously at his waist. "Damn it to hell." He disconnected and went to the door. He peered through the peephole and was surprised to see William, his last Craigslist client, in the hallway.

"Hang on. I'll be right there." Norm turned around, and with his back against the door, slid to the floor.

William continued knocking and calling to him, his voice high-pitched and loud.

"I said, just a minute," Norm answered, while his mind scrambled for what to do. *Stay calm. Think.* He cradled his head in his hands. *Will this day never end?*

He got to his feet and looked around. He considered ducking out the window and using the fire escape to get to the rear of the building. From there he could make a run for it to the car and get away before William realized he was gone. *Bad plan. He'll just come back. Hell, he might even show up at the house.* He set his briefcase on the desk and opened it. He shifted the files just enough so that the butt of the Ruger's grip was barely showing. He pasted on a smile and went to open the door.

"William," Norm greeted the young man. "Sorry about the delay," he said smiling broadly. "When nature calls, you know." He motioned for William to come in but blocked him just inside the door. "What can I do for you?"

"A man showed up at my house today," William said. He fought to slow his breathing. "He wanted to know why I was living in *his* house." He reached for his pocket.

Norm held up his palms and stepped back. "Whoa, there buddy. Let's talk about this."

William pulled out a crumpled paper. "This is his name and phone number. He told me I have twenty-four hours to get out or he'll set my stuff in the street himself. I told him I bought the property from you, fair and square and he said that explains a lot." William took a step toward Norm. "What did he mean by that, Mr. Seitz?"

"Let's go in here." Norm motioned for William to follow him into his office. He turned on his laptop and waited for William to sit down.

William perched on the edge of his chair and leaned across the desk. When he craned his neck to get a better view of the computer screen, Norm angled the machine away.

"I'll pull up your file and we'll see what's going on. It's obviously some paperwork snafu," Norm lied. His mind raced as he tried to figure out how to worm his way out of this one. "Darn internet is slower than molasses," he said. He typed some letters into the search engine to get a 'page unavailable' message on the screen. "Sorry, old man." He turned the computer around to show William. "Looks like we're out of luck for now." He pushed back his chair and stood up. "Give me some time. I can straighten this all out." He extended his hand. "Nothing to worry about, son."

TWENTY-FIVE

It had taken an hour and all of his powers of persuasion for Norm to convince William to leave the office. Still, Norm had to promise to be at the house at seven the following morning and resolve the matter right then and there. He unlocked the file cabinet and pulled out the Kragle file. He found one property where he might be able to move William and his wife. According to Big Roy's intel, the elderly owner had been forced into bankruptcy following a long illness that left him with piles of unpaid medical bills. He managed to hang on to his house but luckily for Norm—though not so much for the owner—the man suffered a brain injury when a neighborhood youth lost control of the drone he was using to survey the neighborhood and the machine bounced off the old gentleman's head. Sadly, he died shortly after leaving his small, brick bungalow sitting vacant for more than a year waiting for the heirs that never materialized.

Norm sipped his scotch. He'd be in serious trouble if William decided to go to the sheriff. He took the Ruger out of his briefcase and laid it next to his drink. With one finger, he spun it around while he tried to figure out what to do next. *The rent will be higher. Bigger place but crummy neighborhood. Still, Bobo didn't teach me the art of the steal for nothing.*

He placed the gun in his top drawer, finished his drink and phoned Little Roy.

The phone rang four times and he was about to hang up when the big man answered.

"Hey," Norm said. He could hear somebody singing, if you could call it that, in the background. "What are you doing?"

"It's karaoke night at Giggle's, " Little Roy said.

"I got a job." Norm paused. "I need you to put the locksmithing skills you learned in prison to good use."

"I can pencil you in for tomorrow afternoon," came Little Roy's garbled response. He called to someone to 'hang on sweetheart.' "I gotta go," he told Norm.

"I need this tonight."

"You're joking, right? It's my night off."

"Every night's your night off. Days too."

"Helluva way to ask for a favor. What is it?"

Norm explained the job. "I'll make it worth your while."

"If you're not there in fifteen minutes, I'm leaving," Little Roy said. "I promised a hot chick the next song."

...

Carin's eyes were red and swollen. She'd spent the last three hours alternately crying and smashing the collection of milk glass the couple inherited from Norm's mother. Carin hated the stuff anyway and this was as good a way as any to get rid of it.

She emptied the last few drops of Merlot into her glass. Colbert was interviewing an actress whom Carin never heard of, but she paid attention long enough to admire the young woman's shoes before her mind drifted off again.

Carin jumped when she heard the garage door open. She sat up straight, smoothed her hair and rubbed her eyes dry. She was ready.

"Be there in a sec," Norm called to his wife as he entered the house from the garage. "I need to get out of these clothes," he called as he headed toward the bedroom, unbuttoning his shirt on the way. "Pour me a drink of whatever you're having, babe."

Norm finished cleaning up and put on a pair of old shorts and a sweatshirt with *University of Cincinnati* in faded letters across the chest. He opened his briefcase to retrieve the gun to put it in the safe. Empty. *The office? Crap. I remember I had it when I was on the phone with Little Roy.* He smacked his forehead. *The desk—I stuck it in the drawer. Damn.* He fished his running shoes out from where he'd kicked them under the bed and found his car keys in the pocket of the pants he'd tossed in a heap in the corner.

"Going out?" Carin blocked his path. She clutched a sheaf of papers in one hand and a glass of wine in the other.

"Yeah. Left something at the office."

"Before you walk out of this house—for the last time, I might add—you care to explain this?" Carin waved the papers at him.

"Look, I'll be right back. Whatever burr you've got under your saddle this time will have to wait," he said over his shoulder as he opened the door. "I really have to..." A piece of the shattered glass crunched under his shoe. "What the hell happened in here?" He looked closer at his wife and the papers she held. "Oh, God." He faced her. "I can explain."

"That's good, because I'm *dying* to hear what you have to

say." The wine gave Carin the courage she needed.

"Let's go in the kitchen and sit down." Norm reached out to take her arm but she jerked it away.

"Come on, babe. I'll make a pot of coffee." He wrinkled his nose and gave a loud sniff. "I know I could use some and from the way it looks—and smells—I think you could too."

"Why? You going to poison *me*?"

Norm took a step backwards. His face registered shock. "Carin, you honestly can't believe..."

"Oh, I can't believe a lot of things, Norm. First, I couldn't believe you planned to go behind my back to use my father's property for some scam you were hatching with Fowler and that low-life Gates. Now, I learn you forged my name and..." She'd sworn she wouldn't let him see her cry but she couldn't hold back the flood of tears. She threw the papers at him and stormed into the living room. She huddled in the corner of the couch and covered her face with her hands, sobbing. When she looked up, her face was stricken. "I don't even know who you are anymore."

Norm's face registered shock. "How'd you...?"

"I found out when I tried to put the house up as collateral for bail money for the Alvarezes. I can't believe you would go behind my back and do such a despicable thing."

"Hold on a minute, lady. Before you go all self-righteous on me, chew on this." Norm felt his anger rise up. His day had already gone into the crapper and this confrontation with Carin was the last straw. He scooped the incriminating documents off the floor and shook them in his wife's face. "You never asked any questions when you were living it up on the money that paid for all this, did you?" He made a sweeping gesture with his arms. "This house, the Harley, a condo in Cancun, the clothes—just how did you think this all happened? You've been living in la-la land and," he bellowed and threw the papers at her, "and, now it's time you climb down out of your ivory tower and find out what real life is like." He sneered and held out his hand. "May I invite you to join me? Let me warn you—you're going to get your well-manicured hands more than just a little dirty."

Sauerkraut ambled into the room and sat on the floor beside his mistress. He looked from Carin to the Norm, a low growl rising in his throat.

Carin stood. She picked up the full glass of wine she'd just poured and threw the contents at her husband. "Get out."

TWENTY-SIX

When Hank arrived at Tippi's room in the ICU, everything was there—but Tippi.

"Hey, Hank." Tippi's nurse tapped him on the shoulder. "I didn't expect to see you up here."

"I can see that," Hank exploded. "Why in the..."

The man's face fell. "Nobody called you? I am so..."

"When did it happen?" Hank was close to hysteria.

"Hank, Tippi's fine." He reached out to steady Hank who appeared on the verge of collapse. "She's great, in fact. She's been moved downstairs to a regular, medical floor. I am so sorry. I thought surely somebody called you."

Hank held back tears and fought to get his emotions under control. Finally, he was able to speak. "I thought for a second I was going to need that bed myself." He nodded in the direction of the empty room. "I think I just had a heart attack."

...

When he stepped off the elevator, Hank followed the din of what sounded like a party coming from what he knew had to be Tippi's room.

150

"Hank's here," Wittekind called above the din.

"Where've you been, buddy? We started the celebration without you," Elrod chimed in.

A roller coaster of emotions made Hank pause in the doorway, his eyes riveted on the pale but smiling face of the woman he loved.

"Go on, Hank." Carin gave him a gentle push.

"Make a path, kids," Amy said.

"Look who finally rolled out of bed," Tippi greeted the latest arrival. "Bend down here," she instructed Hank, "I bet I'll smell pancake syrup on your breath." She reached up and pulled him to her for a kiss.

"Woo woo," cried Wittekind. "Now that's what I call a proper welcome back."

The others clapped and cheered their approval. Hank sat down on the bed, never taking his eyes off Tippi's face.

"Let's give these two some privacy," Amy said as she and Carin ushered the others into the hallway. "I say we head over to the diner for a celebratory lunch. Dessert's on me."

"Let's call our ladies and ask them to meet us there," Wittekind said to Elrod.

"That okay, Amy? It would mean two more pieces of pie," Elrod said.

"Sure, no problem. About time we checked them out anyway. We need to make sure they pass muster." She winked and blew Tippi a kiss as she shut the door behind her.

...

"Okay, Hank, now tell me everything I missed while I was asleep.

And don't leave out stuff because if you do, I'll find out and it won't be good—for you." Tippi crossed her arms and waited.

"Whew, I need a minute to gather my thoughts. You know they didn't tell me you'd been moved and when I went up to ICU and you weren't there..." his voice shook.

"Yeah, yeah. You thought I was dead. Yada, yada, yada. Get over it. I'm alive. Now talk."

"That's not funny, Tabitha. I've been a wreck these past few days. It was touch and go there for awhile." Hank rose and walked to the end of the bed and tried to look angry. Failing that, he turned away and went to the window.

After a long silence, Tippi spoke, "Sorry."

"Okay." Hank moved to the side of the bed and waved his fingers for Tippi to move over. "Scootch."

"Look here, Hank, I'm not up for that. Like you said, I almost died and ..."

Hank threw back his head and let out a loud, belly laugh. When he regained control, he wiped the tears from his eyes. "Oh, Tippi. I have really missed you."

"I know but..."

"I just mean, let me lie down next to you. No hanky panky, I promise." He adjusted his lanky frame so only his rear end hung over the side. "Okay, I'm in—mostly."

Tippi nestled against him. "Now, tell me everything starting with who won the mahjong tournament."

Hank propped his head up on his arm. "You mean you don't remember...?"

Tippi shook her head.

"Then get comfortable. We have a lot of catching up to do."

TWENTY-SEVEN

Velma Gates pushed the control on her new chair to a full reclining position. She tapped the button again and sat upright. She repeated the actions several times before finally deciding on the partial recline. She loved her new chair; the electric control switch, the soft white leather that wrapped around her like a warm blanket and what she referred to as the 'ejector seat' that propelled her short squat body forward to a standing position. Velma tried to conserve energy whenever possible and the chair certainly filled the bill. She usually fell asleep in it, thus saving her the effort of getting up after the news and climbing the stairs to bed. She and Big hadn't slept together in years. He didn't fall asleep until the early morning hours with his nose stuck in one of the books he kept stacked on the bedside table so it wasn't as though her husband even missed her.

She fished in the pocket on the outside of the chair's arm for the remote control. The new 75-inch TV with ultra high definition and surround sound took up most of the wall in the family room. The sound system almost blew out Velma's eardrums the first time she turned it on.

Velma was pleased she'd held her ground against Big's argument over upgrading their cable programming to 'Platinum Plus" and the premium movie channels to boot. She'd pointed out that his vote didn't count since he only watched ESPN and Fox but she lived a much more rounded life (he almost busted a gut laughing when she'd said that) and the Real Housewives of every city in America was only the tip of the reality worlds she lived in vicariously. Big was as tight a man as she ever met in her life so when CLAW handed them the check for putting their land into a trust, Velma threatened him with divorce if he didn't fork over a few thousand to her to spend however she wanted. She decided to reward herself with the TV and the recliner for putting up with him all those years. She had her eye on a mini fridge that would fit snugly beside the chair and still leave her with a nice little nest egg.

She snuggled deep into the cushions and channel surfed until she settled on a re-run of *Keeping Up With the Kardashians.*

"I'm going out," Big Roy called to his wife as he loaded his oxygen tank onto the small dolly he used for traveling.

"Will you be home for supper?"

"I dunno. What're we having?"

"Whatever you bring back," Velma said and turned up the volume on the TV to drown out Big's response. When she heard the door slam, she smiled and opened the box of chocolate-covered cherries she'd hidden under her sweater. *Now this is what I'm talkin' about.*

...

Big Roy drummed his fingers on the conference table in Norm's office. He gave up trying to listen through the wall to Norm's telephone conversation. He'd find out what new scheme the mogul wanna-be was up to soon enough. Roy had his own game plan worked out and now all that was left was a little arm-twisting and he would knock Norm off his high horse into the muck where he belonged, designer suit notwithstanding. Big Roy would show this town he was a man to be reckoned with—no longer the town joke or some dumb hick.

"Afternoon, Roy." Norm pushed up his sleeves as he entered the room and pulled up a chair across from his visitor. "What's up?"

"Well, now," Big Roy drawled, "The gentlemanly thing to do would be to offer me something to drink. Some of that single-malt Scotch you reserve for your special customers sounds real fine."

"Sorry, buddy. I've got another meeting and we have to make this quick. I agreed to see you because you said it was urgent. So lay it out for me."

"Not very hospitable, but okay, I'll cut to the chase." Roy leaned back in the chair and took a cigar out of his shirt pocket. He bit off the end and looked around for a place to spit it out.

"You can't..." Norm stuttered.

Big Roy spit the stub onto the floor. He looked amused as Norm jumped up and dug the discarded bit out of the carpet's deep pile. Finding nowhere to throw it, he stuck the soggy mess in his pants pocket.

"Mind if we move into your office?" Big Roy slid the plastic tubing over his head and draped it around the tank. He cranked the knob to 'off'. "I'm gonna light this thing," he said and waved the cigar under Norm's nose, "and I'd prefer that your pretty face is not the last thing I see before I meet my maker."

The old man shuffled into the adjoining room and took the seat behind the desk.

"Hey, that's my..."

Big Roy waved Norm into the visitor's chair across from him.

Norm slumped into the seat and waited.

Big Roy took his time lighting the cigar and pulled a long draw before he spoke. "Now, here's how I see things are with you, Norm. You're ass-high in debt." He waved the cigar around, knocking ash onto the carpet as he did. "You're living the high-life on a low-life's wallet. I know for a fact, Bobo Fowler is not gonna s t around with his head up his ass for long before he comes after you for what's due 'im." He squinted at Norm and waited for his reaction.

Norm's jaw dropped to his chest, his face paled.

"And besides that, word is your wife tossed you out on your kiester and you're," he glanced around the room as he spoke, "living in these luxury accommodations."

Norm gasped.

Big Roy leaned in. "I see I got your attention."

Norm got up and went into the reception area. When he returned, he carried a crystal candy dish filled with mints, wrapped in silver and tied with blue ribbons. He dumped out the candies and pushed the dish at Roy. "Use this for your ashes, you uncouth son of a..."

"Now, now. Before you get your fancy panties in a knot, I came to offer my assistance."

"Really? You? Help me? That's rich. If I hadn't brought you in, you'd still be selling' apples outta a roadside stand just like that old man of yours." Norm rose out of his chair and pointed to the door. "Get the hell out of my office. You screwed me over once already. What do they say? Fool me once shame on you, fool me twice, shame on me? Well, it's shame on you."

Big Roy didn't move. He tapped his ash into the crystal bowl. "Now that you had your little temper tantrum, *boy*, sit down, settle down and listen real careful because I'm only gonna make you this offer once—even if we are friends and…" he stopped to hack phlegm into a dirty handkerchief. "Water," he barked once he caught his breath.

"The cooler's out." Norm stalled.

"Water, dammit," Big Roy croaked. He sucked in air noisily and his lips took on a blue tint.

"I'll have to go down the hall." Norm reached across the desk and opened the drawer. He kept his eyes on Roy while he pretended to fish around, attempting to push the Ruger out of sight. He retrieved a large wooden key fob stamped with the word *Men* and stomped out of the room.

Big Roy's natural, pasty complexion had returned by the time Norm came back. Roy downed the thimble-full of water and crumpled up the cup. His voice hoarse, he went on, "As I was about to say. It doesn't take a genius to see that you are in deep shit in the money department." He rubbed his palms over the soft leather arms of his chair and looked around the room with a grin like Alice's Cheshire cat. "And I don't need a degree from F.U. to understand that these scams you and me been running is not keeping your fancy lifestyle afloat or gonna go on forever. I mean even that jackass of a sheriff is eventually goin' to find out somebody's selling houses that don't belong to 'em or cashing in on old ladies' life insurance."

Norm balled up his fists and pounded the table. "Why should I trust anything you say, you two-timing', lying..." He cradled his head in both hands. When he looked up, he spoke in a low voice dripping with loathing. "You and me had a deal. We were going to combine your property with Schwab's and with Bobo backing us, we were set to build condos, a golf course, even a Wal-Mart. We were going to make so much money..." His lip curled in contempt. "We could've gone legit. Forget selling houses that aren't ours or putting the squeeze on grieving widows or shaking down geezers hard up for cash. Peanuts. We could've been living on easy street for the rest of our lives." He pounded the desk with both fists. "But noooo— you decided to blow it all for a lousy four-hundred grand." He threw back his head and laughed.

Big Roy leaned back in his chair, puffed on his cigar and waited.

"Four-hundred grand. That's what I get for trying to do business with a stupid, old coot who can't see the forest for—for the apple trees." Norm smacked his forehead with the palm of his hand. "Do you have a clue as to how much I'd already sunk on this project? Greasing Bobo's palms not to mention what it cost me to get a majority on the planning committee who were ready to go against Applebee and vote in favor of the proposed development. Did you think this all just fell into place? You really are a naive old bastard."

The older man snuffed out his stogie in Norm's crystal bowl and sat up. "You done?"

Norm ran his fingers through his hair and nodded.

"I came here like a gentleman…"

"Ha, that's rich." Norm said, looking up.

Big glared back. "I came here as a gentleman," he repeated, "and as your friend." He waited, expecting another outburst. Hearing none, he went on. "You and me had a good run but our days are numbered. I need you to pay me what's owed and I walk outta here for good—maybe not a rich man, but then," he smiled, "I don't mean to be greedy."

Norm did a double take. He tried to hide his relief but something in Big Roy's demeanor, or maybe it was their shared history, made him suspicious. His mind raced.

"I can see you're surprised," Roy said. " It's simple. We close the books on our joint *business* ventures and I keep my mouth closed. I'd like to enjoy the time I have left on this earth before Velma throws dirt over me and spends my hard-earned money on TVs and bonbons." He stood and offered Norm his hand. "I estimate you owe me somewhere in the neighborhood of," he paused to take a pocket-sized notebook out of his jeans. He flipped through pages of numbers. "I show here you owe me forty grand. That sound right?"

"I'll check it against my records," Norm said, thinking it was more, "and send you a check."

Make it a cashier's check payable to Royal M. Gates."

"Royal?"

"You heard right. That a problem?"

Norm shook his head. He got up and ignored Roy's outstretched hand.

Big Roy shrugged and turned to leave. He stopped in the doorway and faced the younger man. "Don't mistake my kindness for weakness, Norm. We had a good run but it's over. Time to move on."

"Right, and I should listen to you because?"

"Look around, Norm. What the hell do you have to lose?"

TWENTY-EIGHT

Hank stuck his head out the window as he backed his SUV into Tippi's driveway, trying to line up the passenger side with the walkway to the front door. The cargo area of the vehicle was full of flowers, balloons and stuffed toys from well wishers during Tippi's hospital stay that completely blocked the rear window.

"You're on the grass. Straighten up." Tippi's voice rose, "You're making tracks in the grass."

Hank pursed his lips and pulled forward, this time over-correcting and driving onto the lawn on the other side of the drive.

"Now you're wrecking the other side. Hold on. I'll get out and direct you." Tippi reached for the door handle when Hank slammed on the brakes throwing her back in her seat.

"We're here," he said brusquely. He took his time unfastening his seat belt, opened the car door and stepped out. He shook out one leg, then the other before walking slowly around the front of the car. He opened the door and reached inside to take Tippi's elbow.

"I can do it," she said, pushing his hand away. "I'm not some old lady."

"And I'm no boy scout," Hank said. "But, I'm much too tired to pick you up off the pavement, although I'm sure you'll give me detailed instructions how to do it." Hank was physically and emotionally exhausted and he was on the brink of losing his temper. From the minute the nurse helped Tippi into the wheelchair for the ride to the door where Hank waited to take her home, there had been arguments and insults about the way the hospital volunteer handled the wheelchair to the way Hank loaded the car, to the route he chose to take her home and lastly, to his driving skill—or lack thereof.

"You drive like an old man." Tippi struggled out of the car and fought to get her balance. She gripped the open door, pretending to examine the tire tracks Hank had made in the grass.

Hank stood by, waiting. "Whenever you're ready."

"If it will put you in a better mood, I will take your arm."

"Thank you so much, Tabitha. It would." Hank winced when ⁻ippi clutched his forearm as she took tentative steps toward the house.

The front door swung open. "Welcome home!" Amy shouted as she and Carin rushed out and wrapped Tippi in an embrace.

"I'll start unloading the car," Hank said, although no one was paying attention. He rubbed his arm and left it to the women to get ⁻ippi inside. He welcomed the help and chided himself on speaking so sharply to Tippi earlier. The whole experience at the center, the deaths of Gert and Violet and almost losing Tippi were catching up with him.

"That's the last of it." Hank set a bouquet of pink and white balloons in the center of the dining room table. He felt like a third—or fourth—wheel. "How about if I make a run to Kroger's?"

"No need, Hank. Check out the fridge," Amy said. "Carin and I already covered that. In fact, how about if you make some sandwiches and coffee and..."

There was silence.

"Make that a pitcher of ice tea," she amended, "and we can all catch up."

...

"I bet you're tired," Hank said after seeing Carin and Amy to the door. He stifled a yawn. "Why don't you lie down and I'll finish cleaning up the kitchen." He was stretched out in the recliner and knew if he didn't get up and move, he'd be the one falling asleep.

"Maybe later," Tippi said. "Something's been bothering me."

Hank sat upright and sprang to Tippi's side on the couch. "What is it? What's wrong?" He took her hand and peered at her anxiously.

"No, nothing physical." She offered him a half-smile. "I didn't want to say anything with Carin and Amy here, but I'm remembering something I heard while I was in the hospital." She wrinkled her forehead. "It had to do with Big Roy, a lot of money and breaking the law."

Hank brushed a stray pink hair away from her face. "Wow. Who was talking?"

"I don't know. I've been trying to remember but I'm only getting bits and pieces." She rested her head on Hank's shoulder. "It was somebody who's in a lot of trouble and has done something bad. That's all I remember."

"Well, let's see. You had an awful lot of visitors. Almost

everybody from the center showed up at one time or another." Hank tried to fight back another yawn. "I'm afraid I'm too tired to think clearly. What do you say we both catch some shut eye and work this out in an hour or so?" He smoothed her hair.

"Okay, but I don't think I'll be able to sleep until I figure this out." She scooted to the edge of the sofa cushion and attempted to stand. "Damn."

"Let me help." Hank stood in front of her and offered both hands to pull her up. "Whew," he said when she was on her feet. "I think you must have gained..." He managed to stop himself in the nick of time.

Tippi surprised him with a hearty laugh. "It's okay. I can honestly say I enjoyed the food. Three meals a day in bed—and snacks. All my friends coming to see me." She sounded wistful. "That part was nice."

Hank put an arm around her waist and walked her to the bedroom. "I think I recall a big box of Graeter's chocolates too." He helped her onto the bed and bent down to remove her shoes. He shut the drapes and patted the covers around her. "Maybe I'll have a piece now," he teased.

"Good luck with that." Tippi turned on her side and immediately fell asleep.

...

The room was in semi-darkness when Hank woke up. He rubbed his eyes and tried to get his bearings. When he attempted to sit up, a sharp pain beginning in the small of his back shot down his right leg. While he waited for the pain to subside, he remembered that he'd intended to lie down in the recliner and close his eyes for a few minutes while Tippi napped in the bedroom. He checked his watch; it was almost six-thirty, three hours later.

The house was quiet. He checked on Tippi who was softly snoring in the same position as he'd left her. *I ought to wake her up.* His stomach growled and he realized they hadn't eaten since lunch. He crept back into the kitchen and checked out the contents of the refrigerator. Hank pulled out a carton of eggs and the ingredients he could use to make omelets. He was chopping onions when he heard the rustling of covers coming from Tippi's room.

"Hang on," he called, wiping his hands on a towel. "Don't try to get up. I'm coming."

Tippi sat on the edge of the bed and rubbed her eyes. "Is it morning?"

"Not yet. It's almost seven—PM." He helped her stand and slid his arm around her waist. The poison had left her with something the doctor called 'foot drop' of her left foot resulting in the toes of the affected foot dragging behind when she walked. The physical therapist had taught Tippi how to compensate so she was able to walk but still needed to regain her strength and balance. A follow-up visit to the physical therapist for a brace was already scheduled.

"I'm making omelets and toast," Hank said. He pulled out a chair at the kitchen table and eased her into it. "What do you want to drink?"

"I'm in the mood for a gin and tonic," Tippi said and grinned. "Must be a bunch of Mormons running that hospital. I couldn't get a cup of coffee, a soda or a highball. Heck of a way to treat a dying woman."

"I don't believe it was because they were Mormons, Tabitha." Hank mixed the drinks and topped off the eggs with a sprinkle of cheese.

When they'd finished eating, Hank put the dishes in the sink to soak, and made two more highballs. He helped Tippi into the living room where he settled her in the recliner so she could put her feet up. "Any more thoughts about what you'd heard in the hospital? Maybe if we start with the people I know came to visit while you were in ICU?"

Tippi sipped her drink and nodded.

"We can rule out hospital staff, I think." Hank swirled the lime around in his drink. "And me, of course."

Tippi nodded. "I'm sure it was a man's voice though." She frowned.

"That's good. Well, let's see. There was me and Grange."

"Applebee?"

"No. He felt terrible about not coming but he had too many bad memories."

"About me?"

Hank chuckled. "Well, maybe, but that wasn't the reason. "You know Applebee contracted polio when he was a kid, right?"

"Yes. When I first met him I asked him if he'd had a stroke and he told me. He didn't elaborate though."

"He was eight at the time. He spent three months in an iron lung at General—now, University—Hospital."

"I had no idea."

"Pretty traumatizing for a little kid." Hank looked thoughtful.

"Anyway, he hasn't been able to set foot—or wheels—in the place since. He said it was okay for me to tell you. He didn't want you to think he didn't want to come. He hoped you'd understand."

Tippi nodded. "I do. I'm glad I know. But," she said, "we still don't know who it was I overheard."

"Hold that thought. Somebody's on the porch." Hank opened the door to find Norman Seitz holding a gigantic arrangement of red long-stemmed roses.

Norm smiled sheepishly and peered over Hank's shoulder. "A small welcome home gift."

Hank turned. "Look what I found..." He stopped cold.

Tippi's face was the color of death. She clasped her hands over her mouth.

TWENTY-NINE

Big Roy Gates instructed Little Roy to pull his pickup beside the loading dock behind the main building of SunDown Ridge Extended Care. He took a deep breath of oxygen before turning off the tank's regulator and removing the tubing and nosepiece. He put a finger to his lips and motioned for his son to exit the vehicle. According to plan, they kept the engine running.

Big Roy carefully opened his door and left it open. He wanted to keep the overhead light on in the cab to allow enough illumination for Little Roy to jimmy the lock to the back door of the building or to make a quick getaway—whichever came first. The eleven to seven shift had just come on duty and Big Roy knew from his own brief incarceration—as he referred to his rehab stint— at the Ridge, the few aides and two nurses on duty would be meeting with someone from the previous shift to review patient charts. He knew he had at least thirty minutes in the clear.

"We're in, Pop," Little Roy said in a stage whisper.

Big Roy patted the bulge in his pants pocket and slipped inside. He hugged the wall as he made his way to the skilled nursing wing of the building.

Big Roy peered around the corner of the hallway where Leon Smears' room was located. This was the most difficult part of his scheme. Leon's room was located directly across from the nurse's station. He hoped he wouldn't be spotted but even if he were, he had a story prepared about being on his way home and deciding to check on his old friend. It wouldn't seem too out of the ordinary since Big had made it a point to visit Leon at least once a week since he'd been admitted to the Ridge, and he had become friendly with the staff.

As he expected, the nurse's station was empty. He hurried down the hall and stepped inside Leon's room. The door was closed when he arrived, but he doubted anyone would notice anyway; it wasn't as if the Ridge attracted any but the bottom feeders of the medical profession. The place had been closed twice before because of Medicare violations.

Big Roy turned on the pocket flashlight he'd brought with him and shined the light on the sleeping man's face.

Leon Smears opened his eyes wide.

"Good evening Leon. I hope I'm not intruding. You're not expecting a pretty nurse to come give you a backrub or something, are you?" He winked.

Leon stared back.

"I'll take your silence as a 'no' then." Roy pulled a chair close to the bed alongside Leon's head. "You up for a little visit?"

Leon blinked once for 'yes'.

"I had a good visit with your daughter-in-law yesterday."

Leon blinked one time.

Big Roy leaned forward and rested his elbows on his knees.

"Nice girl, Carin."

Leon stared.

"I wanted to do something to help her out—now that's she's on her own since she tossed ole Norm out on his can. About time, too, if you ask me." Roy removed two papers from his shirt pocket and unfolded them. "Yep, I bought her old man's farm. Got a good price too." He cackled. "She was anxious to unload the place so sold it for...Well, take my word for it, I got a deal." He folded up the papers and put them back in his pocket. "And, I promised her I'd put one of them land trusts on it—like I did on my place. Already talked with the CLAWs. She and I agreed to split the half-mil or more we'll make on the deal." He laughed. "That was a no-brainer. All because some kind of crawfish lives there will die out if it's not preserved. How do you like those apples? Half a million dollars for a damn fish?"

A gurgling sound came from Leon's throat.

"Norm?" Roy waggled a finger. "Your boy's in the doghouse with the misses. That's why she wanted to sell old Schwab's place so quick. She had to move before her hubby sold it out from under her. Seems your boy was cooking up some shady deal with Bobo Fowler. Had visions of a golf course, a Wal-Mart and rolling around in piles of money." Roy shook his head and wrinkled his nose. "Apple don't fall far from the tree, eh, Leon. Your boy's a bad one. Has you to thank, I guess."

Leon blinked twice for 'no'.

"Well, I gotta be moving on, old friend. Just thought I'd stop in one last time to say goodbye." Roy looked downcast. "We haven't always seen eye to eye but that's all water under the bridge as they say. I'm even gonna let you off the hook for the five hundred you cheated me out of at poker that time." He brightened up. "I remembered how much you enjoyed a good *Jack* and *Coke*, buddy, so I thought you might enjoy a little nightcap." Big Roy took a plastic water bottle filled with amber-colored liquid from his right pocket. He shook the bottle and removed the twist-on cap.

"Now, I know you can't actually enjoy the taste or the feel of the liquid burning your throat on the way down like you used to, but I guarantee it will still have a kick when it hits your stomach." Big Roy held the bottle up so Leon could see. "Cheers, old man. Here's to happy endings."

Big Roy pulled back the covers and uncoiled Leon's feeding tube. Leon blinked over and over as Roy poured the contents of the bottle into the tube.

Roy pocketed the empty container and paused at the door for a final look back. "Yep, bought the farm."

...

Little Roy pulled the truck into the drive-through lane at White Castle. "Give me a Crave Case and a double order of Loaded Fries," he said into the speaker. He turned to Big Roy who was still trying to catch his breath. "You want anything, Pa?"

Big Roy loosened the regulator on his oxygen tank as far as it would go and inhaled deeply. "No way even you can eat thirty sliders," he croaked between breaths. "I'll have two of yours."

"Drink with that?" came the sleepy voice in the speaker.

"Not unless you added Budweiser to your menu," Little Roy said. He pulled up to the pick-up window and held out his hand to his father. "Ante up, old man."

"What for?"

"Consider it a down payment on what you owe me for this job. I got better things to be doin' at two in the morning."

"Yeah, like what?"

"Like sleepin' for one."

Little Roy used Big's credit card to pay for the food. He pulled the pickup behind the building, out of sight of passing motorists. The duo, momentarily quiet, concentrated on eating. The aroma of grilled onions and hot grease permeated the air inside the truck.

Little Roy finished first. "Hand me one of those Buds, will ya', Pop?" He held out his hand to his father who dug through the melting ice in the cooler and came up with a chilled can.

"Remember, we got another job to do and I won't take a chance on you being dulled by alcohol even more than nature already did to you."

Little Roy ignored the remark. He'd heard it all before.

"I'm tired, Pa. I wanna go home."

"Family comes first, boy. Now, shut up and let's get on with it before my tank runs out." Big Roy tightened the regulator again since his breathing had finally returned to normal.

Little Roy started the engine and threw the empty food containers out the window. He pointed the truck toward Main Street and eased out of the parking lot.

...

Big Roy heaved one final, deep breath before he slipped the plastic nosepiece out and wound the tubing around the oxygen tank. He patted the bulge in the pocket of his jeans and opened the vehicle door. "Ready?" he said to his son.

Little Roy nodded.

"Okay, let's do this."

Little Roy burped.

"Real couth, son."

Big Roy swung his legs out of the truck and stretched his back as he stood in his driveway where Baby waited with the ATV.

Little Roy helped his father into the vehicle. A fresh oxygen tank had already been loaded onto the vehicle.

"All set?" Baby asked.

"I'll meet you there," Little Roy said. "Don't start without me."

Big Roy smacked his son on the back of his head. "Drive, moron."

THIRTY

Hank and Tippi sat together on the sofa, watching their guest fidget with his gin and tonic. The clinking of ice cubes was the only sound breaking the uncomfortable silence. Hank cast sideways glances at Tippi whose face at last resumed its normal color.

"Can I freshen that drink for you, Norm?" Hank asked.

"No," Norm said, draining his glass. "I have to get going. Just thought I'd stop by to welcome you home." He rose and started to leave.

Hank followed him to the door. He stood aside to allow him to pass. "Thanks for coming over."

Norm turned around to face Tippi who hadn't moved from her seat. His forehead creased. "I'm glad to see you looking so well, Tippi." He searched for the words, "I bet you're glad you slept through most of that ordeal in the hospital, right? I mean, that was pretty scary stuff." He looked to Hank for help but got only Hank's stony stare for his effort.

"Scary is right," Tippi said.

Norm's expression grew hard. "Then, I'll be seeing you."

Hank watched from the doorway until the lights from Norm's vehicle disappeared from view.

"Well," he said on return, "that was awkward. I want to know why you reacted the way you did. It was Norm you heard, wasn't it? What exactly did he say?"

"I'm going to need another drink first. Martini this time," Tippi said. She held out her empty glass.

"Making up for lost time?" Hank said.

"Mormons, Hank."

Hank stuck his head in the fridge where he could roll his eyes without being seen.

"And while you're at it, throw out those roses. I never want to see Norman Seitz or his stinking flowers again."

Hank was adding ice to their glasses when he heard a noise. "Now what?" He peered out the kitchen window.

"What? What's happening?" Tippi called from the living room.

"Somebody pulled up. I'm trying to make out who it is but...Oh, crap. It's Elrod and Wittekind. Just what we need. I'll tell them you went to bed." He started for the front door.

"No, don't Hank. If anything could cheer me up right now, it's those two characters. I'm tired and a little depressed and I need to put Norman Seitz out of my mind for now."

Hank opened the door before Wittekind's finger reached the bell.

"Hey, buddy," Wittekind said. "Hope we're not disturbing you." He held something in his hands behind his back.

"We were in the neighborhood," Elrod chimed in. "On our way home from our date." He elbowed Wittekind and winked.

"Come in, fellas. Tippi and I were just about to indulge in a couple of martinis. Care to join us?"

"Listen to that. Hank's got all high falutin' on us, Elrod." Wittekind brought out the six-pack of beer he'd been hiding. "Check this out." He held up the carton. "Brewed right here in Cincinnati. Rhinegeist Pale Ale. You take one sip of this…"

"You'll give up martinis," Elrod interrupted.

Wittekind nodded.

"What's going on out there?" Tippi called from the sofa, frustrated at being left out of the action.

"Go on in, guys." Hank took the beer from Wittekind's grasp. "I'll put this in some glasses."

Elrod and Wittekind exchanged glances, helped themselves to a bottle each and filed into the living room.

"Give me a hug, then sit down," Tippi commanded. "Boy, are you two a sight for sore eyes."

"That's a good thing, right?" Elrod asked.

"A very good thing." Tippi embraced each man and motioned for them to take seats on either side of her.

Hank entered carrying a tray with two glasses and the beer the men had brought.

"What's this?" Tippi asked.

Wittekind explained that he and Elrod had taken Pansy and Rosemary to downtown Cincinnati for a ride on the streetcar followed by a stop in the historic Over-the-Rhine district for dinner at the Alabama Fish Bar. "We don't care for the 'Alabama' part because we're in Ohio but…"

"The food is great. I had the perch," Elrod said.

"They give you a lot," Wittekind said.

"And, it's not expensive," added Elrod.

Tippi gave Hank a thumb's-up.

Hank took a sip of beer. "Wow. This is really good."

"Right. After we ate, we took the ladies on a tour of the brewery. They even give you free beer and then we bought some 'cause I was the designated driver so I couldn't have any of the free stuff." Wittekind shot Elrod a mean look.

"I drove last time so it was your turn," Elrod huffed.

Hank jumped in, familiar how these conversations could ramble on into wastelands of minutiae. "Sounds like you and these ladies are getting pretty serious."

"Do you want to tell 'em or should I?" Wittekind grinned at Elrod.

"You do it," Elrod said.

"We're gettin' hitched," Wittekind said.

"Yeah. In two weeks." Elrod said.

"As soon as Norm gets us our money." Wittekind said.

Hank and Tippi exchanged surprised looks.

"Married?" Tippi said.

"Your money? What do you mean?" Hank asked.

"We sold Norm our life insurance," Wittekind said. "We were playing cards with Big Roy at the center, talking about how we wanted to pop the question but we were low on cash, if you get my drift."

"Yeah," said Elrod. "Social Security wasn't designed with love in mind."

"That's the truth," Wittekind said.

"Anyway, that's when Big Roy told us about how Norm could help us out by buying our life insurance. Said he's done it lots of times for other people." Elrod explained.

"Am I missing something? How do you sell your own life insurance?" Hank looked to Tippi who shrugged. He couldn't believe what he was hearing.

Elrod smiled. "It's easy. Roy explained that Norm would give us each ten thousand dollars up front, minus—wha'd he call it, Wittekind?"

"A commission," Wittekind said.

"Right, a commission," Elrod said. "He becomes the beneficiary and we get the cash while we're alive and can enjoy it. Plus, we won't have the premiums to pay."

"'Course, me and Elrod plan on bein' around a long time, don't we buddy?"

Elrod beamed and bobbed his head. "We don't have kids so..."

"Think it's too late?" Wittekind winked.

"*And*," Elrod said, "since we're leaving our bodies to the university, there won't be any funeral expenses."

"Sounds to good to be true," Hank said with a frown directed at Tippi.

"We know. And best of all, you know what they say?" Mr. Wittekind looked from Hank to Tippi.

Tippi squeezed Wittekind's hand. "No, what do they say?"

"Married people live longer."

THIRTY-ONE

"What do you think?" Norm tried to read William's expression as he stood with the couple in the living room of Norm's latest real estate acquisition. The property had been vacant for almost a year while the probate wheels of the great State of Ohio slowly and painfully turned.

"Nice hardwood floors throughout, roof only five years old," Norm lied. He had no idea how old the roof, the furnace or anything else in the house was and, he didn't care. He just needed to prevent William—or the real owner of the last house he'd *sold*—from contacting the sheriff before Norm had a chance to implement his plan.

He patted his pocket. The check from the Vaccaro broad, his passport, and his first-class, one-way ticket to the Maldives, were all there. His briefcase held his bank account number, showing deposits he'd made to the island bank that would ensure him a comfortable life in paradise without those annoying extradition laws. All that was left was for Leon to die and to collect his million dollars from a life insurance policy Norm had convinced him to buy, with himself as beneficiary naturally.

William looked at his wife. "I don't know. Jackie?"

"I love the kitchen. It's so bright. The backyard's really nice too. Big enough for a swing set." She rubbed the tiny bump on her stomach and looked wistful.

"You guys are pregnant? Hey, that's great—congratulations." Norm amped up the enthusiasm. He ran a new scenario through his head. "Tell you what, I was going to have to charge you more for this place because as you can see, it's a lot bigger and much nicer." He swept his hand around the room. "I'm going to suggest you pay me the additional costs up front—that would be forty-five hundred..."

Jackie gasped and gripped her stomach with both hands. "Mr. Seitz, we don't have that kind of money. We had to borrow the down payment for the last house from my father. He's only got his pension from the factory and social security. We can't ask him for more money." Jackie looked tearfully to her husband.

"Hold on, honey. I was about to say," Norm spoke fast. "As CEO of *Money Matters*, I deal in more than just real estate." He looked to William who frowned.

"I also set up annuities—investments—for young families like yourselves." He got out his phone and pulled up the calculator.

William held up his hand. "Stop." He put his arm around his wife's waist. "We want the money back we already paid you. We don't want annuities. I don't even know what that is. We want—no, *need*—a place to live. We're going to be out on the street by five o'clock tonight, Mr. Seitz. We only got that long because the owner felt bad for us."

"I'm real sorry about all this. Damn county. People down there could screw up their own mothers' birthdays. Anyway, hear me out. I want to make it up to you—even though it wasn't my fault." Norm knew he had to make the sale or everything he'd worked for would go up in smoke. "I will take the forty-five hundred dollars you owe me for this place..."

William's jaw dropped. "You're crazy."

"I will take that money and invest it in your baby's...boy or girl?" he asked Jackie.

"Boy. William, but we're calling him Billy." She beamed at her husband.

Her husband stood a little taller.

"I will invest half of your forty-five hundred—that'll be my way of compensating you for your trouble—into a mutual fund in little William's name. I can get you in on a great fund run by an old college friend of mine. Right now, the price is rock-bottom because the *Street* hasn't heard much about it yet. It's all tech stuff including a brand new company that hasn't even gone public. The way the market is going, you'll recoup your investment in no time. By the time you're ready to send Billy off to college, he'll have the pick of any one he chooses. Harvard, Yale—and it won't cost you a cent. Now, wouldn't his grandpa think Billy's college tuition would make a nice birthday present?"

William looked skeptical but Norm sensed he might be weakening.

"I've got my moving guys waiting for my call to go to the other house. They'll pick up your stuff, bring it over here. I'm paying." Norm held out his hand.

William looked at Jackie. She patted her unborn child before she nodded her approval.

Norm took William's proffered hand but before shaking on the deal, he turned to Jackie. "First, better call your dad." He paused. "Say, Jackie?"

She stopped in the middle of dialing.

"It's okay if your dad wants to give me something to invest too. Social Security? That's a joke. 'No security' is more like it."

THIRTY-TWO

Big Roy Gates stood with his children on Bobo Fowler's front porch. He held his finger on the doorbell until the porch light came on and a sleepy Bobo cracked open the door.

"What the hell?" Bobo said through the opening.

Big Roy nodded at Little Roy. The big man put his shoulder against the door and heaved. The door flew open knocking Bobo to the floor. He looked up to the panel on the wall beside the entrance that should have alerted him to the arrival of his unwelcome visitors. The blinking red light that indicated the system was 'armed', was off.

Big Roy followed Bobo's glance. "Don't ever say prison is no place for rehabilitation. Little Roy here graduated first in his class for," Big nodded at the alarm, "all kinds of useful skills."

"What is that gawdawful smell?" Baby chirped as he walked into the foyer. He held his nose and looked around for the source. The other Gates followed suit.

A hairless, pale-skinned creature slunk into the room, ears perked and emerald green eyes surveying the newcomers. The animal farted and rubbed itself against Baby's leg. "Get that stinkin' thing offa me," he screeched. "What is it?" Baby danced and kicked and hightailed it into the living room where he sprang onto an ottoman in the far corner.

Bobo scrambled to get up off the floor. His silk dressing gown tangled around his legs offering his guests a view that made GG cover her eyes with the hand that wasn't holding her nose. When he finally got to his feet, all pretense at dignity lost, he found his voice. "Look what you did." He pointed to a fresh turd in the spot where Baby had been standing. "You scared my cat."

"Cat?" Little Roy said. He scooped up the animal and held it at arm's length for inspection. "Is this thing really a cat?"

Bobo grabbed the animal and held it close to his chest. He rubbed its head with his chin. "Yes, it's a cat. A very expensive cat, aren't you, Milton?" Bobo kissed Milton on the head and held him tight. "Daddy forked out a thousand smackers for you, didn't he, baby?"

"A thousand bucks? I can't believe it. A thousand bucks for a damn cat?" Little Roy repeated.

"Shoulda got one that didn't stink," GG waved her hand in front of her nose.

"He's a Sphynx. The breed…wait a minute," Bobo said, "never mind all that. What the hell are you *people*," he snorted, "doing in my house in the middle of the night?"

"Well, technically, it's morning," Big drawled. He leaned in to get a closer look at the cat that looked back. "But your question is a good one, isn't it, gentlemen?" He smiled benignly on his offspring.

GG huffed, "And, ladies, pop."

Big ruffled his daughter's hair. "Right. And lady."

Baby Roy returned with a bottle of beer. He took a long swig and wiped his mouth on his sleeve. "I needed that." He peered suspiciously at Milton, then changed the subject. "Man, you should get a load of this guy's kitchen. He has one fridge with nothin' but wine and another one with all kinds of fancy beer I ain't never heard of." He held it up to the light. "This is a good one." He waved the bottle under Little Roy's nose. "I think we just found ourselves in the Promised Land." He emptied the bottle and dropped it on the floor.

"Do you have any idea how much this rug costs, you uncouth hillbilly?" Bobo stooped to pick up the discarded bottle. He attempted to mop up the splatter with the bottom of his robe. Milton tried to help by licking up what he could.

Baby picked up the cat and nuzzled its head. "You got good taste, Milty. I think you and me are gonna get along after all."

"Alright, that's enough," Big Roy stepped in between his son and Bobo. "Let's go into the living room and talk."

"We've got nothing to talk about," Bobo shouted. "Give me back my cat and take you and your disgusting brood out of here now or I'm calling the sheriff." He walked to the door and held it open.

Little Roy, who had been standing next to his father, silently removed Bobo's hand from the doorknob and closed the door. He looked down on the other man. "My daddy told you to move. Either you do that yourself or I'm gonna pick you up by the scruff a' your scrawny, chicken neck, and move you. Now, lead the way."

186

Baby Roy was waiting for them in the living room. A purring Milton licked the rim of his beer bottle.

A fire sputtered in the limestone fireplace that comprised an entire wall. A giant moose head, mounted above the mantle, presided over the room. A white, bear skin rug, head and all, rested in front of the grate where GG lay down and closed her eyes.

Big Roy settled into a corner of the soft leather sofa that wrapped around the table. Little Roy escorted Bobo to the seat beside his father and plopped his portly self down, cushioning Bobo between the two Gates.

"Let's get down to business," Big Roy said. "You may be aware, Bobo, that I recently purchased the Schwab place from Carin Seitz."

Bobo's mouth fell open. No words came.

"I'm surprised that surprises you," Big Roy said. He made a slicing motion across his throat when Baby started to interject. "I took you for a man who kept his finger on the pulse of this town."

"Ha," Baby said.

His father shot his son a look that silenced him. "As I was saying, with Schwab's place, I now own near to six hundred acres." He smiled. "You see, I need to make sure my children are taken care of after I'm gone."

"Don't worry, Pop, the state will be takin' care of Little Roy. I hear they's keeping his cot warm over at Warren Correctional."

"Shut up, moron," Big Roy barked.

"I don't know what any of this has to do with me," Bobo said.

"I'm gettin' to that," Big said.

"I'm gonna have a look around, Pa," Baby Roy said. He tucked the cat under one arm and plucked another beer off the table. "I bet this guy's got lotsa neat stuff in this place." Milton farted again and licked Baby's cheek.

"Get that stinking beast outta here." GG sat up and rubbed her eyes. "I think I'm gonna puke."

Bobo smiled.

"We're going, ain't we Milty?" Baby said as he started to leave. He stopped and turned back. "Hey, Bobo, you got one a' them pictures with the dogs playin' cards? I love that. Remember, Pa? We saw one in that real fancy motel that time we went to Dollywood." He started for the hall.

"Kids," Big Roy smiled indulgently after his youngest child.

Baby Roy stuck his head around the door. A grin lit up his pasty face. "Man, I'm gonna love it here."

THIRTY-THREE

"As ordered, homemade chocolate-chip cookies and coconut-chocolate chunk ice cream." Bob Applebee wheeled into the kitchen, a canvas bag loaded with Tippi's favorites sagged from the arm of his chair. "And this one's for the guest of honor," he said lifting up a pink gift bag tied with a large pink and white bow. Bob's two-year old Jack Russell terrier sat on his lap, a fringed, pink blanket draped across her stout little body.

Tippi hobbled forward to greet him. She pounded down her pink, leopard-colored walking stick with each step. When she stooped to hug Bob, she was intercepted by Frenchie, who shot her long, pink tongue into Tippi's open mouth. "Phewy, damn dog." Tippi reared back, wiping dog spittle off her face. "Some things never change," she said sternly, a small smile lighting up her cobalt blue eyes.

"I'll take this," Hank said, coming in behind his friend. He removed the sack from Applebee's chair and put away the contents. "No samples," he warned Tippi who stood by watching. "You can open this," he said taking the gift bag from her, "in the other room—once you're sitting down."

"There's a bowl of food in there for Frenchie," Bob said. He lifted the dog from his lap and set her down beside his chair.

"And, I need everybody to get out of the kitchen." Hank turned Applebee's wheelchair around, took Tippi's cane and instructed her to push Bob into the living room. "You two catch up and let the others in when they arrive. I set out snacks and drinks to ward off starvation and to keep the hungry horde at bay until dinner's ready. Frenchie and I got things covered in here." He watched to make sure the pair made it safely to the sofa before closing the doors. "Alright, buddy," Hank said as he set out the dog's bowls, "Here's yours, now I need to get this show on the road."

...

"Great meal, Hank." Mr. Wittekind wiped his mouth and helped himself to another cookie. Pansy, sitting next to him, whispered something in his ear. Wittekind colored and slipped the cookie in his pocket. "I'll save this for breakfast." He looked at Pansy who nodded her approval.

Tippi beamed at the head of the table. She wore her gift from Applebee, a pink sweatshirt with *Don't Call Me Sweetie* in a glittery silver arc across the chest.

Elrod, his hands clasped in his lap, beamed across the table at Rosemary.

Amy and Carin rose and began clearing away the remains of the meal. "Don't say anything important until we get back," Amy said. She wagged her finger at the sheriff who was trying to open the button on his pants without anyone noticing.

"Hurry up," Wittekind said. "Me an' Elrod got an announcement." He winked at Tippi.

Hank returned with a pot of coffee in one hand and Frenchie

under his other arm. "Think it's past this one's bedtime," he said. He placed the animal in Applebee's lap where she immediately burrowed under her blanket and fell asleep.

Once the table had been cleared and everyone had settled down, they looked to Hank expectantly.

"Thank you all for coming," he began. "Tippi and I wanted to express how much your all being there these past couple of weeks has meant to us." He looked to Tippi who nodded and made a circling motion with her hand for him to move it along. "The boss is saying I should get to the other matter we wanted to talk about." Hank took a deep breath but before he could speak, Elrod jumped up from his seat.

"Me and Wittekind's gettin' married."

Sheriff Grange looked over at Amy who raised her eyebrows and shrugged.

Mr. Wittekind rose and patted his friend's shoulder. "He means, that him and me are getting married," he offered as if that explained it. He looked around the table for a reaction. Seeing only puzzled faces, the light bulb suddenly went on in his brain. "Oh, no," he reddened. "We're not getting married, I mean we are," he sputtered, " but, not to each other." He looked to Hank for help.

Hank laughed until tears came. When he finally regained his composure, he explained, "What the guys mean, is that these young ladies," he raised his cup to Pansy then Rosemary, "have agreed to take on what I can only imagine will be the extraordinary challenges of marrying Elrod and Bernie." He grinned at Mr. Wittekind. "Please join me in raising a toast to our old friends—

and our new ones."

Hear, hear," Applebee said, as the others took turns hugging the happy couples.

"Now, if everyone could take your seats," Hank began. "We have something serious…"

Tippi interrupted with an ear-shattering blast on the whistle she wore on a silver chain around her neck. They'd taken it off when she was in the hospital but now that she was home, she told Hank it was back on for good.

"Listen up, people," Tippi's voice boomed above the others'. "We've got other stuff to tell you about and Hank needs your full attention."

"Thank you, Tabitha," Hank said wryly.

When Hank, with verbal cues and reminders from Tippi, finished telling the others what Tippi had overheard Norm say at the hospital, the room was still.

All eyes turned to Carin who dropped her face in her hands. Soft sobs rippled through her body.

"Carin, none of us believe you knew anything," Applebee said. Pansy, sitting beside the distraught woman put her arms around Carin. "He fooled you along with the rest of us."

Carin looked around the table, her face streaked with tears, her mascara pooling around her eyes. "I've learned a lot of pretty bad things about my husband…about Norm. But surely you know what he said was just exaggeration. I mean, people say stuff like that all the time. I won't believe that." She looked for affirmation but seeing none, she left the room.

Tippi struggled to her feet and hobbled around the table

beside Hank. Hank hurried to slide a chair under her. "Tell them the other part, Hank."

"Do you want to tell them?" Hank looked at Elrod, then Wittekind.

Elrod looked puzzled.

"The insurance?" Hank prodded.

"You mean how Norm bought our life insurance?" Elrod said. He looked to Wittekind who nodded and shrugged.

"Big Roy's the one who told us about how we could get our hands on some extra cash, you know, for the wedding and stuff. He called it a *life settlement.* We checked it out. We even saw some real famous celebrities in an ad..."

"And we called the company from TV ourselves," Elrod added.

Wittekind nodded. "They said it's a great deal for seniors. Like those reverse mortgages."

"That's right," Elrod said. "Roy made a good point. Said we'd been paying all those premiums for years and for what? We couldn't enjoy it if we were dead. And by selling to Norm, we'd be dealing with one of own, a friend, you know? Win-win, he said." Elrod looked to Wittekind for confirmation.

Wittekind's face fell. "Do you think it was all a scam?"

Hank nodded. "The business is legit, although barely. It's a racket. These guys are known to leave out the part about their fees—usually thirty percent—and that the seller will have to declare the money as income and pay taxes on it. That leaves..."

"Pennies on the dollar." Wittekind's hands shook as he lifted his water glass to his mouth. "And," he said, "Norm gets a big payout when we kick the bucket."

Elrod turned to his bride-to-be, "I feel like a fool."

Rosemary wrapped her arms around him.

"The guy's a pro," Hank said. "You couldn't know. None of us guessed he was anything but an obnoxious jerk."

"Where does Roy fit in?" Applebee asked.

"It looks like he just finds potential clients and Norm pays him a commission on actual sales. We don't know for sure." Grange went on, "Not illegal, that we know of. Yet."

Amy squeezed his arm. "Tell them what else, hon."

"The station took a call from a man who said his daughter and her husband had purchased a home through the rent-to-own listing on Craigslist. He said he'd loaned the young couple ten thousand dollars for the down payment and first month's rent. The seller was Norman Seitz."

"That doesn't sound suspicious. What made him call you?" Applebee asked.

"After they moved in, a man showed up on his daughter's doorstep asking why they were living in *his* house. Said he'd call the department if they didn't vacate the property immediately. Wish he had."

Amy rubbed his shoulder.

"Anyway, the guy's son-in-law goes to see Seitz who apologizes all over the place. Blames it on county record-keeping and offered them another home, for an additional fee, naturally. He then tried to sell them an annuity for the baby they're expecting at Christmas. William, the son-in-law wanted nothing more to do with Seitz and wanted their original ten grand back but the wife had fallen in love with the new place. She persuaded William to go along."

"And they called dad for another loan," Hank said.

"Right. Thank goodness, dad refused. That's when he called the station."

"What happens now?" Applebee asked.

"I've got the family coming in to give a statement tomorrow morning." He directed his next question to Elrod and Wittekind, "I have to ask, did you already...?"

Mr. Wittekind nodded forlornly. "We cashed the checks. We wanted a nice wedding and a honeymoon." He gazed sadly ay Pansy. "I'll understand if you want to call it off. You deserve better...'

"Not on your life, mister," Pansy said.

THIRTY-FOUR

Big Roy turned to Bobo whose face had been drained of every ounce of blood. "I guess my boy let the cat out of the bag."

Bobo stared back, slack-jawed.

"See, I got three kids and I guess it's no secret they aren't the sharpest bunch, mentally speaking."

Bobo snorted.

"Right. You do understand," Big Roy said. "Well, with Schwab's place and mine, that would take care of two of them when me and Velma are gone, but that leaves one little Gates out in the cold. Understand?" Big checked to see if he was getting through to Bobo, who sat next to him.

"My Pa asked you a question, man. "You understand what he's gettin' at, right?" Little Roy put his big hands on either side of Bobo's face and forcibly moved the man's head up and down.

Bobo squeaked something unintelligible.

"Say again," Little Roy asked, putting his ear to Bobo's lips.

"Was that a 'yes'?" Little Roy said.

"Un uh," Bobo whispered.

"Let me explain," Big Roy said. "You see, I've been communicating with the CLAWs." He paused to see if Bobo was following.

"I did hear that," Bobo said.

"I won't go in to details—saving crawfish, farmland, creeks, perpetuity, and so on. Bottom line—and I know the bottom line is what's important to a sharp businessman like yourself, isn't that right?"

Bobo's mouth hung open. He nodded.

"Well I don't give a tinker's damn about saving fish or the godforsaken dirt people around here call farms. To paraphrase the great Robert Frost, I'm done with apple-picking now. However," he stroked his chin, "when the government handed CLAW a blank check to dole out to upstanding citizens like myself to stop the big, bad boogiemen like you, that being *developers,*" Big stopped to get his breath before he went on, "I held out my hand and a big, fat check fell right into it."

"Ma bought herself a big, new flat-screen TV," Baby Roy chimed in and, pointing to Little Roy and GG, "we's all goin' to Disney World. We're leaving' tomorrow. I'm gonna get me one of them hats that look like Mickey's mouse ears." He hopped from one foot to the other. "And, they'll even sew my name on it." He grinned, his missing front tooth of no concern. "I need another beer." He hopscotched his way toward the kitchen.

"She should have used the money to buy him a tooth," Bobo said.

"You're probably right," Big Roy conceded, "but none of the kids ever been past Gatlinburg and their ma thinks it's time they see the world."

"You're crazy, old man," Bobo said. "If you think for a minute

I'd sell…"

"Maybe you're not understanding me," Big Roy said. "I'm not *asking* you to sell me this place. I'm telling you that you will." Big picked up a silver cigarette case from the table. "May I?" he asked Bobo. He didn't wait for an answer, putting a cigarette into his mouth and lighting up. He studied the ornate engraving on the case and slipped it into his pocket.

"Then," Big Roy picked up where he left off, "I put your property—now *my* property—into a land trust, take CLAW's cash and," he grinned, "I got a new house, a hundred sixty more acres and the government paid for all of it. I think it's what you money guys call *leverage*—not a dime outta my own pocket. Isn't that a hoot? "

Bobo looked at Big Roy with a hint of admiration when he said, "I should have partnered with you instead of that loser, Seitz. But," his voice grew hard, "hell will freeze over before I sell you my place."

"Don't you go disrespectn' my Pa." Little Roy grabbed Bobo by the black, shoe-polish colored hair that curled over the back of his collar, and attempted to yank the man's head backwards. Instead, Little Roy was staring at a cue ball and holding a fistful of hair.

Baby Roy had come back into the room just in time to witness Bobo's big reveal. He doubled over with laughter, managing to eke out the words, "Bro, you snatched ole Bobo baldheaded."

Meanwhile, Little Roy had hurled the offensive hairpiece across the room. He studied the palm of his hand, then wiped it on his pant leg. "Damn grease all over my hand. What the f do you put on that thing?"

Bobo leaped up and dashed across the room to retrieve his hair but Baby got to it first. He held the piece above his head.

"Over here, Baby," GG was on her feet, hands outstretched.

Bobo jumped and tugged at Baby's arm.

"*ENOUGH,*" Big roared, getting to his feet.

Everyone stopped and looked at Big.

"Leave the man some dignity," he commanded. "Give that back," he ordered his son.

Baby at least had the decency to look ashamed when he handed Bobo his hair.

Bobo placed the toupee back on but somewhat askew causing him to keep swiping the bangs out of his eyes.

"If everyone's done playing," Roy admonished his children, "let's get down to the business of why we're here."

...

Little Roy rolled the oversized roller bag to the driveway and hefted it into the back of the ATV Baby had parked behind of the house.

"Okay in there, Milty?" Baby opened the top zipper a crack and put one eye to the bag." We'll be home soon. You take a little ...oh, crap. You gotta stop passin' wind or my Pa's gonna drop you in the pond. Got it?"

GG arrived wearing white coveralls. She pulled off her plastic gloves and cloth shoe covers and stuffed them in the plastic bucket with her disinfectant.

"Clean up complete?" Big asked his daughter.

GG nodded.

"Got the keys and the alarm code, Baby?" Big Roy asked.

"Yep. Wanna keep my new digs protected from the bad guys." Baby laughed at his own joke.

"Who says you get this one?" GG snapped. "I think I…"

"Shut up, both of you," Big said. "We still got work to do and there'll be plenty of time for fighting' when we're done and in the clear." He inhaled deeply on the oxygen tubing that he'd put back into his nose.

"What about him?" Little Roy gestured at Bobo who, hog-tied and with duct tape over his mouth, lay in the grass trussed up like a scrawny Christmas goose. Little Roy had finished the job by wrapping duct tape under Bobo's chin and around the top of his head to secure his hairpiece.

"Load him in the trunk of his car," Big Roy instructed.

"Where we takin' him, Pop?" Little Roy slung the wriggling man over his shoulder and carried him to the Mercedes where GG waited for them.

"Downtown. I reckon ole Bobo hasn't handed over everything. That crummy little safe he hid behind the moose—really, Mr. Obvious?" he said to Bobo, "was just a tease. The real money, the documents I need, have got to be downtown. Isn't that right, Bobo?"

Bobo squirmed and shook his head as hard as he could within his restraints. He uttered guttural sounds that sounded like *fork poo.*

"Fork poo?" Baby got up in Bobo's face. He looked from his father to his brother. "What's he mean by *fork poo*? I don't get it."

Little Roy dropped Bobo into the trunk and shut the lid. He looked at his brother and sighed. "You ain't got the sense God give a flea." He turned to Big Roy. "What now, Pa?"

"Now, Baby takes the ATV back home and waits for my call. Can you do that, son?" he asked Baby.

"I'm on it, Pop." Baby fired up the vehicle, gunned the motor and took off.

THIRTY-FIVE

William, Jackie and Jackie's father were exiting the station when Mr. Wittekind and Elrod arrived to give their statements. Jackie's father spoke briefly with the men before escorting his daughter and son-in-law to his car.

Wittekind and Elrod watched the trio drive off. Elrod took a deep breath and put his hand on the door. "Ready, buddy?"

Mr. Wittekind nodded. "Let's get this over with."

"Morning, guys," Sergeant Ed Waller greeted the men from behind his desk. "I'll tell Deputy Potts you're here." He pointed to a table in the corner where a shiny new coffee machine stood. "Help yourselves." He disappeared down the hall.

"Check this out," Elrod said, inspecting the machine. "This is one of those machines that makes your coffee one cup at a time. Hot chocolate too if you want. See?" He held up a stainless steel contraption loaded with plastic cups, each with a different colored lid. Elrod selected one of the pods and placed it in the machine. Within seconds, the aroma of fresh-brewed coffee filled the room. "This is great," he said, sipping the hot beverage. "I think I'm going to put this on my list of stuff people can give me for a wedding present. You should ask for one too." He took a seat next to Wittekind who stared at the floor.

"You okay, buddy?" Elrod asked.

Wittekind looked up and shook his head. "Not really."

"Look, I know this business with Norm's got you down. It's got me down too. But," he sipped his coffee, "the sheriff's gonna nail the crook, we pay back the money to the insurance company and we're no worse…"

"I don't have it," Wittekind interrupted.

Elrod frowned. "What do you mean, you don't have it?"

Wittekind rose and turned his back on Elrod. "Have you gone deaf, man? I don't have the money. It's gone. Spent. All of it."

Elrod stared blankly at his best friend. His mind raced. He knew Wittekind to be careful with his money; some of their acquaintances at the senior center said he was tight, but Elrod never saw it like that. He knew his friend had come from a large family, ten kids in all, and his parents, having lived through the Depression, made sure they all knew the value of a dollar. This revelation that he'd already spent the entire windfall was totally out of character. Elrod was shocked. He didn't know what to say.

Deputy Moira Potts came through the locked door that separated visitors from the rest of the station. Only suspects or citizens coming in to report crimes or file complaints were allowed inside.

"Sorry to keep you fellas waiting," Moira said. She held open the door and motioned for the men to follow her to a private room. Mr. Wittekind elbowed his way past Elrod and sank heavily into a seat. Moira looked questionably at Elrod who returned her gaze with a shrug and a shake of his head as he took a seat on the other side of the table.

...

Moira knocked on Grange's office door. She could hear him finishing his phone call and waited until he called for her to come in.

She took the seat facing her boss and laid two police reports on his desk. "I've got Elrod and Wittekind's statements, boss. I feel so bad for them. What Norm did, sheriff, might be legal but it's still wrong."

Grange picked up the reports and scanned them. When he'd finished, he pushed his glasses atop his head and leaned back in his chair. He lifted the leg with his new knee and gently placed it across the corner of his desk, rubbing it as he spoke. "That was Mary Schmidt on the phone letting me know Violet was also a victim of Norm's insurance scheme. Mary thinks Violet intended to surprise her with that river cruise down the Rhine that the senior center is planning in the spring. Mary's eightieth birthday is next year and Violet had been hinting that she had something special planned. Yesterday, when Mary was cleaning out Violet's drawers, she found a folder with the trip itinerary and a receipt for..."

"Let me guess," Moira said. "Ten thousand dollars."

"Twenty," Grange said. "When Mary phoned the insurance company she learned that six months ago, Violet sold her policy to..."

"Norman Seitz."

Grange nodded. "Seems his investment netted him two hundred grand in under six months."

"Not a bad return, Moira said, "Especially if you rig the odds."

"And Big Roy?"

"Right now, I'd say Roy was acting as Norm's agent at the senior center. At least, he's the one who approached Wittekind and Elrod with an offer they couldn't refuse." He grunted as he lfted his sore leg off the desk. "The question remains, why wasn't there a similar deal made with the Schwab's or were their deaths, or Gert's anyway, simply the result of being in the wrong place at the wrong time?" He stood up and put on his hat. "And, is there a connection between what happened at the mahjong tournament and these insurance deals?"

Moira sat up straight and put on her uniform hat. "What do you want me to do, Sheriff?"

"Let's go back to the beginning, starting with what happened at the mahjong tournament." Grange looked grim. "The evidence against the Alvarezes is awfully thin. Let's dig into their story some more."

THIRTY-SIX

It was still dark when the Gates family arrived at Fowler Tower. Big Roy grunted for his son to drive around to the back of the building. Big had scouted the place out earlier in the week and located a security gate in back with a driveway leading to an underground parking garage. In the course of his research, he learned that the space had been used during prohibition to receive and store liquor that was sold to local saloons. It also connected to a labyrinth of underground tunnels that offered safe passage to the ladies who worked the brothels in Goose Down's flourishing red light district back in the day. The school uniform factory continued to operate on the upper floors but the real money was made below street level under cover of night. Roy knew it was the perfect place to unload the bundle wriggling about in the trunk of the vehicle and also provide the means by which three of the four persons arriving there would make their escape. The fourth soul was slated to make his departure by another avenue.

Little Roy pulled up to the gate and punched in the security code Big had persuaded Bobo to relinquish. The gate slid open and Little Roy eased the vehicle down the slope into the cavernous garage. By the time he'd parked and helped his father out of the car, the entryway was closed and locked behind them.

GG emerged from the back seat and stood next to Big Roy. "How much longer is this gonna take?" she whined. "I'm tired of cleaning up after you people and I need my beauty sleep."

"If there was less complaining and more moving, we'd be done by now," her father said. He walked to the back of the car. "Get him out and take him upstairs."

Little Roy opened the trunk and hoisted the squirming Bobo over his shoulder. "Get that, sis," he told GG indicating the open trunk.

GG grabbed a white plastic bucket holding the supplies she'd 'borrowed' from the hospital. She slammed the trunk shut.

"Maybe they didn't hear you down in Cincinnati," her father barked. "Let's move." Big Roy shone his flashlight in front of him until he found the elevator. "Over there," he pointed the light and led the way.

...

After several unsuccessful attempts, Big Roy succeeded in finding the key that unlocked the door to Bobo's office. He pocketed the key ring and led his little party inside.

"Put him in there," he said, pointing to a room off to the side where a large leather chair reigned behind a polished, mahogany desk. "Untie him and for crying out loud, take that tape off his head and straighten out his hair. No need to humiliate the man."

Little Roy untied Bobo and GG unwound the tape holding the toupee.

"It keeps slidin' off, Pa," GG said. She spit on her fingers and rubbed the saliva around the top of Bobo's baldhead. She placed the toupee on as straight as she could and pounded it with her fist. The hairpiece slid to the side and clung there above his ear.

Big Roy slapped his forehead and took the seat across from Bobo. "Sorry about that," Big apologized. "As you can see, I'm fighting an uphill battle. They got their mother's brains, for sure."

"Yeah, whatever. Now, you hilljacks need to leave," Bobo growled. He started to get up.

"I'm going to ask you to stay seated," Big Roy said quietly. He nodded at his son.

Little Roy took a stand behind Bobo, placed his meaty hands on Bobo's shoulders, and pushed him down into his chair.

"Good," Big Roy said.

Bobo rubbed his shoulder. He looked up at Little Roy. His hair fell off.

"Lord, save me," Big Roy closed his eyes and looked heavenward. It was a full minute before he was able to speak. He took a deep breath. "I'm sure we're all tired and want to get this over with."

"I'm calling..."

Little Roy knocked Bobo's hand away as he reached for the phone.

Big Roy reached into his pocket and pulled out the Ruger. He pointed it at Bobo. "My normally tolerant nature is beginning to fray, Mr. Fowler. So," he crossed his legs and balanced the hand holding the gun on his knee, the barrel trained on Bobo, "here's what we're going to do. First, you're going to unlock your desk, your file cabinet and your safe. Understand?"

A stricken Bobo stared at the gun.

Big Roy nodded at his son. "I asked if you understand, Bobo."

Little Roy grabbed Bobo by the ears and bobbed his head up and down.

"Good. Next, you are going to sign over your property to me." Roy unfolded a yellow paper that he took from his pocket. He laid it in the desk and smoothed out the creases. It was a blank deed that he's taken from Norm's office. It was already signed and notarized by Norman Seitz.

Bobo's jaw dropped. He looked at the deed then Big Roy. "But how?"

Big Roy shrugged. He removed a Mont Blanc pen from his pocket, wiped it on his shirt and laid it in front of Bobo.

"You'll never get away with this, Gates," Bobo said. He signed the document and glared at his captor.

"Oh, I wouldn't bet on it," Big said.

...

Bobo Fowler sat at his desk. He surveyed the files and loose papers scattered in front of him. "Alright, Gates," he directed his anger at Big Roy. "You got it all; the deed to my house, my cash." He turned to Little Roy who thumbed through the banded stacks as he put them into the cloth bags GG had brought along. "Now get the hell out of here." His last comment was more of a plea bordering on hysteria than a command.

"One more thing before we go," Big Roy said. "Fowler University."

"Yeah, what about it?" Bobo became defiant. "Totally legit."

"Well, we could argue that but I don't really care one way or the other," Roy said. "Norm Seitz is in to you for some money for his," Big Roy paused, "um, degree. Am I right?"

"Yeah, so?"

"Norm and I are business partners, of a sort," Roy added. "So I need you to consider his outstanding debt to you, paid in full."

"Not gonna happen," Bobo said. "Besides, how am I supposed to live since you've taken everything...?"

Big pursed his lips.

Reality dawned on Bobo like the sun rising over the horizon on a chilly winter morning. "Surely you don't, you aren't..." Bobo stuttered.

"Let's not make this difficult," Big Roy said, his voice low.

Bobo looked at the gun, then into Roy's cold eyes. "Wait. What if?" Bobo's look turned sly. "What if I told you there's something else?"

Roy laid the gun on his leg. He massaged his fingers that had grown stiff. "What?"

"Besides the F.U debt, Norm owes me—that is me and my partners—three hundred thousand for what was supposed to be a golf course on Schwab's property."

"And mine, I believe," Roy said wryly.

"Right," Bobo conceded. "But, I'd be willing to sign all of that debt over to you if you let me go. I walk out of here tonight, you take everything and you never see or hear from me again."

"Interesting proposition but Norman Seitz doesn't have a pot to pee in. What good's his debt to me?"

"Well, as soon as his old man croaks, he's set to get a million bucks on the policy he took out on him a few years back when he got the ALS diagnosis. That should be more than enough to pay you —with interest." Bobo knew he was fighting for his life.

Big Roy smiled slow and wide. He winked at Little Roy who remained stationed behind Bobo.

"Already accounted for, Bobo."

Bobo thought hard. He'd been holding back the last ace he had up his sleeve. Lucky for him, one of his *associates* had connections to the world-banking network. He took a deep breath and prepared to roll the dice.

Big Roy re-positioned the gun. "Spit it out, man."

"Do you know about his stash in the Maldives?"

THIRTY-SEVEN

Sheriff Grange knocked on the front door and stood back. He heard a jumble of voices and listened as footsteps grew closer. The sheer curtain on the glass panel bordering the door was pushed aside and Grange saw the telltale red curls of Carin Seitz appear then disappear as the curtain was dropped back into place.

"Pete," Carin snapped, cracking open the door.

Behind her, Grange could see Victor and Arcella Alvarez huddled together, watching. A backpack and a pile of clothes sat beside them.

"Somebody going away?" Grange nodded at the scene behind Carin.

"Oh, just come in," Carin huffed. She pushed open the door and marched off. She stood next to the Alvarezes, her arms crossed across her chest and her face angry. "What do you want?"

Sheriff Grange removed his hat and nodded to the frightened pair who had stepped back when he entered. "How you folks doin'?"

"How do you think they're doing, Sheriff?" Carin moved in front of the couple to shield them from the visitor. "They've been accused of murder on purely circumstantial evidence—evidence that wouldn't have held water for a second if they were white, I might add—thrown in prison and allowed to rot…"

"It wasn't prison, Carin and…"

"Save it, Pete. This is a travesty of justice and you damn well know it." Carin's green eyes, like two Jalapeño peppers, burned into the sheriff.

Grange motioned to the couch. "Could we sit a minute and talk?"

Carin turned to Victor who had his arms wrapped around his sobbing wife. "Victor?"

Victor nodded and led Arcella to the sofa where she buried her face in her husband's chest, her sobs beginning to ease into soft sniffles.

The sheriff selected an armchair across from the couple. Carin reluctantly moved to a seat beside Arcella.

Grange coughed. "I'm glad you were able to make bail," he said, directing his gaze at Victor.

"You aren't here on a goodwill mission, sheriff," Carin barked. "Cut to the chase and tell us what it is you really want."

"Okay," Grange said. He leaned forward in an attempt to make eye contact with Victor. "There was a question that you refused to answer for the grand jury."

Victor squeezed his wife hard and waited.

"I'm going to approach it from another angle, okay? I know you and Ernie fought over the sale of some property you wanted to buy from him to build a house on."

Victor stared back.

"That's on the record so we don't need to re-litigate it."

"English, Pete," Carin said, crisply.

"Right, sorry," Grange said.

"Is okay. I know it," Victor said. He took his arms from around his wife and sat up tall.

"You went to El Gris Ganso after the fight and started drinking."

Victor kneaded his hands in his lap.

"That's all a matter of record," Grange said. He added in a kind tone, "Look, Victor. I'm not here to judge. I get it. You were fighting for your family. It's what a man does."

"Yes." Victor shoulders relaxed a tiny bit.

Grange noticed and chose his next words carefully. "I'm going to tell you what I think happened next."

Carin took Arcella's hand and held it with both of hers.

"I think Big Roy Gates approached you that afternoon at El Ganso and offered you a deal too good to refuse."

The Alvarezes sucked in a collective breath.

"My deputy spoke with Velma Gates yesterday."

Arcella gasped.

"It's okay, Mrs. A." He offered a weak smile of reassurance. "That day at the Ganso, Big Roy offered your husband a job working for him and Norman Seitz to fix up property for them to sell." He didn't wait for confirmation before he continued, "Roy told Victor to keep Mr. Schwab in the dark about their arrangement or the deal was off."

Arcella looked puzzled. "In the dark?"

"Sorry," Grange said. "I mean, you and Victor were instructed not to tell the Schwabs about Victor's little *arrangement,* right?"

Arcella nodded.

Grange picked up his story and went on. "Big Roy came to your home, brought the money, and told you it was an advance for the work you would be doing. He probably told you to keep the cash available, suggesting that you hide it somewhere in the house so as to avoid questions from the government if you were to put it in the bank."

"Is that true, Victor?" Carin asked.

Victor nodded.

"Then, Norman Seitz called you and said he heard you were looking for a house, right?"

Victor's mouth dropped.

"And I bet he also told you, he knew of a place and it just so happened that ten thousand dollars was exactly all that was needed was a down payment."

"Si."

"That was the money we found when we searched your place, wasn't it?"

"Is that true, Victor?" Carin leaned across and placed her hand on Victor's knee.

"Yes," Victor whispered so softly Grange wasn't sure that's what he heard.

"Yes?" Grange repeated.

"Mr. Norman said I couldn't tell a soul or I'd get sent back. I was so scared." He turned to his wife, tears filling his eyes now too. "I'm sorry."

"You're the victim of a couple of very slick con men, Mr. Alvarez." Grange rubbed his knee and grimaced. "And if it helps any, you're not alone."

THIRTY-EIGHT

"No funny stuff." Little Roy stood behind Bobo, the Ruger jammed into the small of the man's back. "Open it slow and look natural." He straightened Bobo's hairpiece and motioned for him to open the door.

"What the hell is so important I gotta come over here in the middle of the night?" The burly man stood in the hallway outside the office. He towered over Bobo at six-foot eight and easily carried his three-hundred plus pounds, at least half of which looked like it was in the biceps that bulged under his Ohio State tee shirt.

"You know I wouldn't call if it wasn't an emergency." Bobo stepped back to let the man barrel inside.

"Who the hell are you?" the newcomer barked when he saw Little Roy.

Little Roy shoved Bobo aside to reveal the gun, now pointed at the big man's chest. "Let's just say I'm a friend of Bobo here," Little Roy leered. He matched the newcomer in girth if not in muscle, but he was the one with the gun.

The giant scowled around at the little crowd before striding to the chair where Bobo had curled up. He stood over the sniveling man. "What the hell is this, Fowler? Is this one of your sick jokes?" He reached down and pulled Bobo to his feet.

Bobo's knees shook so hard they gave out, and he collapsed in a heap.

"Now look what you done," Little Roy said. He gave Bobo a nudge with his size thirteen shoe.

"Marion, I'm sorry. These guys are..." Bobo whimpered.

"Marion? Your name is Marion?" GG howled. She sprang from her seat. She stood next to the giant and looked him up and down, the top of her head reaching only as high as his massive chest. "Excuse me for asking, but why did your momma give you a girl's name? You some kind of big sissy?" She poked him in his rock-hard side then took a step back. "Wow."

"You finished, girlie? Got any other names you wanna call me before I squish you like a bedbug? Because you're gettin' under my skin."

"Uh, no." GG said. She twirled a strand of her hair in her fingers and batted her eyes. "You single?"

Marion snickered. "You're not my type." He turned to Little Roy. "Put that damn gun down, son, or I'll break your arm when I take it from you."

Bobo curled tight into a fetal position on the floor. "Just do what he says, Marion. The big lug's gonna kill us."

Marion looked at Little Roy. "That right? You gonna kill us?" As he spoke, his right arm, like a lightening bolt, sliced into Little Roy's forearm. With his other hand, he reached out and caught the Ruger. He stepped back and turned the gun on Little Roy.

Little Roy sank to his knees clutching his arm. His eyes pinched shut, he wobbled briefly before sinking onto the floor. A moan thick and guttural echoed through the room as the others watched in silence.

Big Roy closed his eyes. He sat behind the desk, not moving.

Marion reached down with his free hand and jerked Bobo up from the floor. He tucked the gun in his pocket and looked around. "Let's all pretend we're civilized. And you, over there behind the desk," he said calmly, "tell me why I'm here playing 'chicken' with these losers when I should be back in my nice, warm bed?'

Big Roy, eyes still shut, swung one leg, then the other, off Bobo's desk. He stretched his neck, moving his head from side to side, then in a circular motion. When he was done, he lifted one shoulder, then the other. He opened his eyes to stare across the room at the giant. "I'm sorry, we haven't been properly introduced. Bobo, where are your manners?"

...

Marion pushed back his chair. He got up, poured himself a mug of coffee, and surveyed the other occupants of the room. Only Big Roy remained awake and vigilant.

"You really think you can pull this off?" Marion asked Big. 'Pretty ballsey. Wish I'd thought of it." He downed his coffee and poured another cup.

Big Roy shrugged.

Marion squatted in front of Big Roy so they were face-to-face. "I'm just about finished," he said with a nod at the computer on Bobo's desk. "Now, we need," he took a long drink then set his mug on the floor beside him, "to discuss how you are going to compensate me for my work this evening."

Big Roy raised one eyebrow but said nothing.

"A sharp fella like you had to know I didn't agree to help you out of the goodness of my heart. As you can see," he waved to Little Roy, who had moved to a corner of the room cradling his swollen arm, "I could have walked right out of here, or called the police. Any number of options were open to me. But, I like you, old-timer. And," he looked toward Bobo and heaved a deep sigh, "I'm ready to retire. Me and Fowler had a nice run, but I saw the writing on the wall even before this little party."

Marion put his hands on his knees and pushed himself upright. "So, here's where we stand. I'm in the Maldives account, *your* new account is ready to receive the transfer so we've almost reached the finish line." He stifled a yawn. "I still have to write the last bit of code that will make you a very rich man—another half-hour's work and it's done."

Big blinked and waited.

"Now, I know a shrewd guy like yourself can understand that I'm going to need a little something for my efforts. After all, I'm no social worker." He rubbed the small of his back with both hands. "Nor do I have a death wish."

Big remained stone-faced and returned a one-shoulder shrug.

"So, here's how we're going to play this." Marion took the Ruger from his pocket. He removed the mag and emptied the chamber, placing the ammo back in his pocket. He looked around the room until he spotted the scarf GG had tossed on the floor beside her. Using it to wipe down the weapon, he handed the gun to Big Roy. "I believe this is yours." He grinned. "Personally, I have no use for 'em." "Hold on," he checked his phone. "Thought I heard incoming."

Big Roy laid the Ruger on the arm of his chair. "What do you want?"

"I'm going to walk out of here…"

Big shook his head and coughed into his hand.

"Old man, listen up because I'm only going to say this once— and let me remind you that your weapon is empty, your new bank account is empty and as you can see," he smiled across the room at Little Roy holding his arm that was swollen and turning purple, "I have a way of making my point."

Bobo, who had been trying to remain invisible for the past few hours while Marion worked at the computer, uncurled himself from his seat and sidled across the room to stand behind the big man. He poked his head out from behind the human shield. "Yeah, Roy. Me and Marion are walking' outta here with our share or we're going to the sheriff."

Marion heaved a sigh and rolled his eyes. He reached back and pulled Bobo from behind him. "Sorry, buddy," he said, gripping him by the arm. "As of now, I'm working alone." He turned his attention to Big Roy. "He's all yours." And with that he shoved a terrified Bobo at Roy's feet.

"Now, old man, you ready to listen?"

Big Roy sighed. "Do I have a choice?"

THIRTY-NINE

The sergeant hung up the phone. "Damn."

"Problem, Ed?" Deputy Potts stopped on her way to the copier. She set a stack of papers on the counter and propped herself on her elbows.

"The sheriff is trying to track down Judge Foley for a warrant for Norm's office and the good judge is on a canoe trip somewhere in the Canadian Rockies."

"Leave a message at his hotel."

"Good idea, deputy, except he's camping with his son in a place accessible only by helicopter. His assistant says they left yesterday morning and won't be back for forty-eight hours." Ed looked grim, then brightened. "Say, deputy, how about if I make those copies for you and you tell the sheriff..."

"Ever hear the words 'when hell freezes over'?" Moira chuckled, packed up her stack and hurried away.

Sheriff Grange stepped into the hallway. "Ed?" He could use the station intercom but preferred the old-fashioned way.

The older man sighed. He went through the back room that opened into the hall next to the sheriff's office.

"We got the warrant?" Grange asked.

"No. Sorry, boss. Do you want me to call downtown? Maybe somebody else..."

Grange waved him off. "No good. We'll wait. I want Foley because he's familiar with the situation and he knows Seitz from the Planning Council."

"Right, boss. I'll let his office know to call as soon as he gets back. Anything else?'" Ed started back when the phone rang.

"I'll get it in here." Grange headed back inside. "I'm expecting a call." He closed the door behind him and reached for the phone.

"Thought for a minute you guys closed up early and went home," the coroner's familiar voice was on the line.

"I wish," Grange said. "What's the word, Zenobia?"

"Leon Smears was poisoned. Arsenic. Like the others."

...

The BCI tech stepped into the hall where Grange waited. She pulled off her face mask and shook off the cap that covered her short, blonde bob. "This is one for the books, Pete. I admit, I'm stumped."

"I'm not surprised." Worry lines etched the sheriff's eyes. "This case, or should I say these cases, have been one, big Chinese puzzle." He motioned for the tech to move to the side so he could lean against the wall and take some weight off his knee. He'd been on the go all morning and it hurt like the devil. What he really wanted was a steaming hot mug of coffee, his easy chair and an afternoon of college basketball watching the Cincinnati Bearcats.

"What did you find?"

"I didn't find anything." She rubbed the bridge of her nose

where her bifocals left a crease. "There's nothing. No fingerprints, no hair, no DNA. It's sterile—like no one—including your corpse—was ever there. Nursing staff said it's their policy to sterilize patient rooms immediately after they're vacated in preparation for the next resident. Keeping beds full at all times is what this business is about."

Moira Potts arrived in time to hear the end of the conversation. "More bad news, boss." She scanned the notes she'd made on her iPad. "None of the staff saw anybody coming or leaving Leon's room last night. The shift nurse reports that the usual staff meeting began around 10:30 and typically lasts for an hour or so depending on new admits, deaths, doctor calls and the like. Also," Moira checked her notes, "it was one of the aide's birthday, there was cake, so the meeting may have gone longer than normal. She says she left around midnight and didn't notice any unusual activity or unfamiliar vehicles in the parking lot, but admitted she wasn't paying particular attention to anything but 'getting the hell out of there'. Her words, boss."

"So the killer knew the usual routine giving him plenty of time to kill Leon and leave without anybody the wiser." Grange looked from his deputy to the tech.

"Somebody like his son?" Moira said.

Grange said nothing.

"I'll go over my findings with my team again when we get back to the office," the woman said as the two other BCI techs exited Leon's room.

Grange and Moira watched the investigators pack up their gear and leave the building.

"You ready to go too?" Grange asked Moira.

The young deputy ran a red, white and blue painted fingernail lightly across the screen of her tablet. "There's something else, Sheriff," she looked toward the front of the building where BCI loaded their gear into a state vehicle. "When I asked the day nurse who found Leon how Norm took the news, she looked real funny. She said, and these are her words, "'Mr. Seitz said, break out the champagne, toots, and wish the old sot a speedy bon voyage— straight to hell'. "

FORTY

Big Roy and Marion stood in the hallway outside Bobo's office. "You drive a hard bargain," Roy said. He thrust his hands in his pockets and rocked back on the heels of his boots.

"You're pretty sharp for an old geezer," Marion said. "This deal will make you a nice little nest egg, even after I take my share."

"You mean your share and then some."

"My expertise doesn't come cheap." Marion patted both his pockets, bulging with bundles of some of the cash Big had removed from Bobo's safe. "I'll text you once I'm outta this podunk town. Then I'll finish your job."

"How long?"

"Twelve hours."

"Good." Big Roy studied the other man's face. "I don't suppose you'd tell me where I can reach you? You know, in case I had something else?"

Marion laughed. "Our business is finished, Gates." He did a quick check of his phone, clapped Big Roy on the shoulder and walked to the elevator. He punched the 'down' button and waited. "Almost forgot." He reached in his pocket and pulled out a single

226

bullet he'd taken from the Ruger and tossed it to Roy. "I expect you'll need this."

...

"We almost done?" GG stifled a yawn.

Big Roy sat across from Bobo. The former tycoon of Goose Down sat at his desk with his face in his hands, his bald head shone in the light.

"Just about." Big Roy sat across from Bobo. He loaded the single shell in the Ruger and pointed it at Bobo.

"Here's what you're going to do, Fowler. Call Seitz and tell him he needs to get over here right away. Say you've had second thoughts and you have a deal for him. Tell him you'll meet him here in one hour and if he's even one minute late, the offer goes away. If he presses you, say the deal you're offering will make him double what he'd have made on the development project. He's a greedy bastard, he'll bite."

Big Roy took a pink jar out of his pocket and held it up to the light. He unscrewed the lid and sniffed the contents. "Smells like somethin' your cat may've expelled." The gold lid sparkled when he wiped it with a tissue before setting the jar on Bobo's desk.

"We parted on, hmm, should I say, less than favorable, terms? He won't buy it," Bobo said. His voice shook.

"Then it's up to you to sell it."

"You're gonna kill me anyway. Why should I help you?"

"Because he screwed you over like he done half this town. You can be the guy that takes him down."

Bobo cradled the receiver under his chin before he dialed. "You don't have to do this," he said, tilting his head at the weapon.

Roy tossed the pistol from one hand to the other. "Well, think about it, Bobo. You get Norm up here. I only have one bullet."

. . .

Bobo hung up the phone. "He's on his way."

GG entered the room wearing a white tyvek suit. Plastic gloves, paper shoe covers and bonnet completed the outfit. "I'm all done in there, Pop."

Big nodded. "You called your brother?"

"Baby's in the garage with Little Roy."

"You wait in the other room until I call you."

GG cast a look at Bobo and left. She shut the door behind her.

Big Roy rose from his seat, the gun at his side. He folded up the contract between Norm and F.U.C.R. that had been lying on the desk and tucked it inside his shirt.

Bobo watched, wary.

"That cat o' yours?" Roy asked.

Bobo flinched. A tear crawled down his cheek. "What about him?"

"Milton, right?"

Bobo nodded, frowning.

"Milton—Paradise Lost." Big aimed and fired.

. . .

Big Roy's sons gathered around him beside the Mercedes. They watched GG, still gowned in her cleaning attire, finish wiping down the door on the driver's side.

"Group cheer," Baby called when she was done.

"Oh, geez," Little Roy complained, placing his good hand atop his brother's. GG added her gloved one and Big joined in, smiling indulgently.

"Who dey?" Baby started the cheer familiar to Cincinnati Bengals fans. "Who..."

"That's enough, people," Big said. "Let's get out of here." He led the trio to his truck where Baby had parked it beneath the dim glow of the red Exit sign. Big Roy took a seat in back where he gulped air from his tank. GG slid in beside him

Baby hopped into the driver's seat leaving Little Roy to crawl into the front seat beside his brother, cradling his arm that had swollen to twice its normal size.

When Big Roy finally got his breath and was able to speak, he smiled benignly on his children. "Good work, tonight. I'm proud of you."

GG reached over and laid the back of her hand on her father's forehead. "You feelin' alright, Pop?"

Big sucked in another gulp of air. "Moment's passed." He felt for the empty Ruger nestled against his hip. "Hand over that bag, son," he said, patting Little Roy on the shoulder.

Little Roy groaned as he reached for the fat paper sack on the seat between him and Baby and tossed it over his shoulder to his father. "I need to go to the hospital first, Pop. I think my arm's busted. I can't feel my fingers no more an..."

"Quit whining," his father barked. "When we get home you can put some ice on it and you'll be fine. "We show up at Memorial row and we might as well go straight to Grange and tell him what we done. Is that what you want?" Big placed the gun in the sack and rolled the top closed.

"Yeah," Baby chimed in. "You and your little bump ain't gonna get in the way of me and Disney World." He looked wistful. "Yep, a couple a' hours and I'll be in the happiest place on earth, shaking hands with Mickey and Winnie-the-Pooh. I love Winnie-the-Pooh."

"They ain't real, numbskull," GG snarked.

"Whadda *you* know? They're as real as you," Baby shot back, turning in his seat.

"Look out! Red light," Little Roy shouted.

Baby turned around just in time to bring the car to a screeching halt in the middle of the intersection.

Little Roy slammed into the dashboard, his injured arm taking the brunt of the impact. The big man clutched his arm and howled in pain. His face turned gray in the dim light of breaking dawn. "I'm gonna puke," he groaned.

"Put the window down and stick your head out," his father said. Big tapped Baby on the shoulder. "Pull over there, son." He pointed to a narrow alley that ran alongside Norm's office building. "Turn off the headlights and keep the truck running. This will only take a minute." He stepped out and wrenched open the front passenger door.

"Dammit, old man." Little Roy caught himself just in time to escape falling onto the pavement.

"Hurry up, boy. Get me inside."

FORTY-ONE

Norman Seitz checked his glove compartment for the Ruger. *Damn. I must have left it at the office.* While he sat in his car across the street from Fowler Tower, he debated whether he should go back and get the gun. *Better just go inside and see what new scheme Bobo has up his sleeve.*

He entered the lobby and was waiting for the elevator when he heard the wail of sirens. Two sheriff's vehicles and a fire truck screeched to a halt in front of the building. Norm dove behind the reception desk in the center of the room just as Deputy Moira Potts, followed by two other officers, charged inside and up the stairs.

Now what? Norm ducked down and waited. He raised his head and peered around. Another deputy stood outside guarding the entrance. *Damn. How'm I going to get out of here?* Norm crouched lower and crawled to where he could get a better view of the rear stairs. He remembered what Bobo told him about his underground garage that connected to a labyrinth of tunnels under the streets of the town's business district. That was in better times when the two were on friendlier terms. *Like it or not, Fowler, you're gonna save my ass.*

He checked the lobby. It was empty. He figured if he could reach the back exit leading to Bobo's garage, he could follow one of the tunnels leading to a street access several blocks away. He'd worry about his car later.

...

Sheriff Grange was beginning an interview with Tippi Mulgrew. He wanted to get the threats Norm made against Bobo Fowler and Big Roy down in writing before he asked his deputy to bring him in. Added to that, he wanted to know where Norm was the night of Leon's murder, and what Norm stood to gain from his father's death. He hoped the fact that Leon was poisoned like the others would help clear the Alvarezes, since even the wiliest murderer would be hard pressed to murder an old man in a nursing home while incarcerated. *Maybe we're beginning to get somewhere.*

Sergeant Ed Waller knocked on the sheriff's office door and cracked it open. "Sorry to interrupt."

"Hang on," Grange called. He tapped his finger on the legal pad. "Keep writing, Tippi." He motioned to his officer to wait for him in the hall but left the door open so he could keep an eye on his witness.

"Boss, we have a problem." Ed glanced through the door at Tippi whose attention was riveted on the words she scribbled onto the paper. Hank, who, in his role as chauffeur, waited in the corner engrossed in a crossword puzzle. "Boss?" Ed creased his forehead and tilted his head at Tippi.

"It's okay," Grange said.

The older man hesitated. He hated bringing the sheriff more

bad news. The events of the past several weeks were clearly taking their toll. He dove in, "The security guy at Fowler Tower called. He said when he arrived this morning, he went through his normal routine, checking each floor, making sure everything was in order."

"Do I want to hear this?" Grange watched Tippi furiously filling up the pages of the legal pad.

"I guarantee you don't, but here it is anyway—Bobo Fowler's been shot. He's dead."

"What?" Tippi jumped up, knocking over her chair. "Norm killed Bobo? Oh, my God. He said he'd do it and he did."

...

Norm reached the safety of his office out of breath and out of sorts. He locked the door behind him and turned on the television for news about what was going on at the Tower. He started toward his office when he spotted an envelope on his assistant's desk. The return address indicated it was from Leon's insurance company. *Finally, some good news for a change.*

He used the Keurig to make himself a cup of coffee and settled down behind his desk. He anticipated the check inside that would secure a comfortable life in the Maldives, confident that with Leon's million-dollar insurance benefit in addition to the cash he'd stashed in the island account, he would never have to work again. He chuckled at applying the word 'work' to what he did. *But, 'scam' is such an ugly word.*

Norm opened the envelope carefully and shook the single, folded letter. *Hmm, no check. Must be the notice of the award.* He scanned the short message, then read it again. *What the hell?*

The letter stated that in regard to his inquiry about Leon Smears' insurance policy, he, Norman Seitz, was not listed as Mr. Smears' beneficiary and they were very sorry for any misunderstanding. It went on to state that the company was legally bound to follow their client's instructions and could not, naturally, offer any further explanation or information about the matter which was officially closed.

That lying, no-good excuse of a father had actually removed him as his sole beneficiary?

Norm rose out of his seat and screamed into the empty room, "Leon, you dirty S.O.B. You screwed me over one last time, didn't you?" One last, royal fu..." He slapped his forehead. *Royal? It can't be.*

"Gates."

He jerked open his desk drawer and breathed a sigh of relief seeing his gun and passport undisturbed. He checked the gun chamber, then the clip; it was ready to fire. He placed everything in his briefcase. *Royal my ass. We'll see.*

Norm went to his safe and squinted into the dark hole. He staggered backward then peered inside again, unable to believe or comprehend what he saw, or rather didn't see. The two hundred grand in cash from Violet's life insurance was gone. All that was left was a hundred dollar bill sitting atop a single piece of paper.

The room spun around him. Gripping the paper, he swayed unsteadily across the room to the Eames chair, where he sank into the soft leather. *No, it's not possible. How?* He read over the document, a printout of his Maldives account. He looked again.

"No! It's not possible!" Someone had drawn a large, red happy face over the columns of figures. A single transaction showed under today's date; a withdrawal of every penny he'd squirreled away. He was broke. Worse than broke considering the massive debt he'd accrued.

He sat in stunned silence. Finally, shaking off his stupor, he rummaged through his desk until he found the book of matches Roy had left after his last visit. He took one last look at the document then struck a match and touched it to the paper. The fire crawled across the page. *Up in flames—like my future.*

He stumbled drunkenly out of the room and paused in front of the television monitor. Onscreen, the camera homed in on a podium behind a bank of microphones where an official announced the momentary arrival of Sheriff Grange. The subject—the murder of local businessman, Bobo Fowler.

Norm's jaw dropped. *Bobo—murdered?* He stared at the screen where reporters jostled one another for position. Norm couldn't believe it. It wasn't much more than an hour before he'd spoken to him, agreed to meet him to talk about some new scheme. Then, when the sheriff's people showed up, his only thought was getting out. As he'd sprinted away, he'd wondered if there'd been a break-in or if maybe Bobo had had a heart attack, but murder? No way. *What if I walked in while the killer was there? I could have been murdered too.*

He watched as Sheriff Grange stepped forward and briefly described the scene in Bobo's office earlier that morning. He concluded by adding there would be a reward for information leading to an arrest of the killer.

"Better if you offered a reward to whoever finally murdered the little weasel," Norm snarled at the images on the screen and punched 'off' on the remote.

Norm took a long look around his office at the expensive furnishings; the gold-plated sign on the door that read *Money Matters, LLC,* above his name, the view of Goose Down that once held such promise and the large photo of him standing beside Bobo, accepting his certificate from Fowler University. "Time for me to blow this town," he said aloud. He ran a hand through his hair and folded his overcoat over his arm.

He picked up his briefcase and pulled the Uber app up on his cell. The door to his office swung closed behind him.

FORTY-TWO

"Up here," Velma called to Big from the upstairs bedroom. She was bouncing up and down on an old hard-sided suitcase to force the latches shut. "Send Little Roy up. I need a hand."

"I ain't got a hand, Ma," her eldest son hollered up the stairs. "Bobo's guy broke my arm, and Pop won't take me to the hospital. I think I'm getting gangrene."

There was a minute of silence before Velma yelled back, "Did ya' break your legs too? "Cause if not, drag yourself up here and help me—or you can forget about Disney World."

Big Roy caught the end of the conversation. "Let's get this show on the road, people," he barked. "Little Roy, help your mother. Baby, GG, you got your stuff loaded up? We gotta roll."

Baby joined his father. He wore a Mickey Mouse t-shirt and pulled a roller bag that was unzipped about an inch at the top. "I'll load this…'

"There better not be a cat in there," his father said, eying the bag suspiciously.

Before Baby could protest, a loud screech followed by a roxious gas emanated from the suitcase.

"Pop, we can't leave Milty here by hisself. He'll die of lonesomeness. Besides," Baby wheedled, "if Grange comes pokin' around and finds him here, he'd wonder how come we got him. An' Bobo dead and all."

Big thought about that for a moment and hoisted his oxygen tank onto his shoulder. "Then he rides with you. Your cat is not stinkin' up my trailer. Besides, your Ma and I showing up at the Villages with a vehicle that smells like toxic waste would not be a good way to impress our new neighbors."

Velma appeared dragging her suitcase. "Got my chair and TV tied down good?" she asked Baby. "I expect them to get there the same way they left—got it?"

"Don't worry, Ma." GG patted her mother's head. "I'll make sure these boys stay in line."

"Your truck gassed up, Baby?" Big asked.

"Yeah, Pop. Me and GG'll take turns driving since Little Roy's still whining' about his arm."

"I'd like to…" Little Roy glowered at his brother.

"Shut your mouths, morons," Big Roy snapped at his offspring. "I'm leaving. Anybody want to come?"

Four heads bobbed in unison.

"Next stop—the happiest place on earth," Baby Roy called as he skipped out the door.

FORTY-THREE

Sheriff Grange arrived at Fowler Tower just as Zenobia Hachett exited the County Coroner's van.

"Sheriff, we have to quit meeting like this."

"Got that right. I'm wondering what happened to our nice, quiet little town where the only crimes we had to worry about were speeders, drunks and high school seniors tipping cows after homecoming."

"I hear you," Zenobia said. She opened the door and motioned for Grange to go inside. "Ever think about retiring, sheriff?" Zenobia flashed her county badge at the security guard. She followed Grange into the elevator.

"Funny you should say that," Grange said, watching the number of each floor tick upward. He stepped back to allow Zenobia to exit first. The sheriff nodded to the waiting emergency personnel as he guided the doctor through the narrow hallway to Bobo's office. "Retirement is definitely on my radar. Amy tries to be subtle about bringing it up." He smiled thinking of his petite nemesis. "She knows how much I love this job but..." he shrugged and accepted the shoe covers Zenobia offered him. "For now, duty calls."

Deputy Moira Potts greeted her boss and the coroner at the door. "Looks pretty straightforward. Gunshot to the forehead. BCI is on the way but our guys are saying the place is clean."

Grange did a visual sweep of the room when his eyes landed on a familiar object; a pink and silver jar gleaming from its perch on the corner of Bobo's desk. Beside it lay a pen. "Zenobia?"

The coroner looked up from the floor where she crouched over the body.

Grange slipped on a pair of plastic gloves he carried in his pocket and held the jar up so Zenobia could see. "Look familiar?"

Zenobia stood up to get a closer look. "Wow."

"What are you two talking about?" Moira said. "What's in the jar?"

"A very expensive lip balm," Grange said.

"Specially made for a certain customer by a Chinese guy in Philadelphia," Zenobia added, grinning.

"I don't get it," Moira said. She reached out a gloved hand to examine the jar more closely.

Grange shook his head and held it out of her reach. He waggled his fingers. "Bag."

Moira handed him an evidence bag. "How do you two know about this? And who travels from Goose Down to Philadelphia for lip balm, for cryin' out loud?" Her eyes flashed, understanding. "Norm."

"You got it, deputy." Grange dropped the jar into the bag and ran his fingers along the top to secure the seal. He handed it to Moira. "Take this downtown and log it in as evidence. Bag that pen too. Might mean something to somebody. Have whoever's on the desk get a warrant for Seitz' office—and his house."

"But the Judge..." Moira started.

"I know. It'll slow us down. Just get anybody who's available." The sheriff's eyes had regained their sparkle, his shoulders were straight, and his voice sounded strong and sure.

"We're going to nail that S.O.B."

...

Sergeant Ed Waller had set the wheels of the law in motion. He'd called in two off duty deputies to come in to wait for the warrant. He wanted them ready to go as soon as it arrived. In addition, he'd placed an ABP for Norm that included airports in Cincinnati, Dayton and Columbus. With assistance from area law enforcement agencies, the interstates and major roads in the tristate were under surveillance. Besides Norm's Hummer, the bulletin included Carin's Harley and the ubiquitous blue Honda CRV.

Tippi Mulgrew waited until Ed finished with his last phone call. "Here's my statement." She thrust a handful of yellow sheets at him. "Hank's taking me to the diner for a late breakfast in case you need me. I haven't eaten for hours and this," she nodded at the papers in the Ed's hands, "has given me a heck of an appetite."

Ed squinted his confusion at Hank who stood by impassively. 'Okaaay." He placed the papers into a folder and scribbled something on the tab before setting it aside. "I'll give it to the sheriff as soon as he gets back. Thanks." He turned his attention to an incoming call.

"I'm taking you to breakfast?" Hank said, gripping Tippi's elbow and propelling her forward. His car was parked in the spot designated Handicapped. He opened the passenger door and helped Tippi inside, adjusting the foot that still sported a plastic boot.

"You know, Hank," she said, when they had both secured their seat belts.

Hank waited. He suspected he was in for another 'teachable' moment. "Yes?"

Tippi tried to decide if he was being sarcastic before she went on. "Handicapped is a very objectionable term. I've decided to take the matter to City Council to have it removed from all the signs in Goose Down. After I've fixed it here, I'll take the movement nationwide—maybe the world."

Hank gripped the steering wheel. He rested his head on his hands and shut his eyes. "I'll bite. Why is 'handicapped' objectionable and what should we say instead?"

"Since I've become, umm, shall we say, one of the physically inconvenienced, I have decided to become an advocate for myself, and other people too, of course," she added after a slight pause. She pulled down the visor and checked her makeup in the mirror. Satisfied, she continued, "As you know, Hank, I am widely considered to be an excellent wordsmith."

"I learn something new about you every day. I mean, I know you are a woman of considerable talents," Hank said. His voice was muffled since he had not lifted his head from the steering wheel.

"Thank you. I know. Anyway, as I was about to tell you, the word *handicapped* is considered one of the top ten worst words to call disabled people. Google it."

Hank said, sitting up. He reached across the seat and straightened the silver whistle around her neck. "That's interesting," he said. And meant it.

Tippi slapped his hand and motioned for him to start the car. "Breakfast." Her stomach, as if on cue, growled.

Hank pulled out of the lot and headed for the Down Town Diner. The drive would only take about ten minutes as it was mid-morning and traffic was light.

Tippi told him to watch out for a kid riding his bike on the sidewalk and settled back in her seat. "The reason I haven't gone to council yet," she said, picking up the thread of the conversation, "is because I haven't decided on a good substitute. I mean 'physically challenged' is too cumbersome. 'Disabled' is almost as bad as 'handicapped'. 'Differently abled' is kind of okay and some people like it. I just wish I could come up with something snappier, more colorful that still gets the message across." She sighed deeply and looked down at the plastic contraption designed to keep her foot from dragging.

"I have no doubt you'll figure it out."

She studied the passing landscape. "Yeah."

They drove on in silence until they came to Bobo Fowler's property. "What do you think will happen to his place?" Tippi asked.

Hank slowed the car to a crawl. They tried to get a look at the house but trees blocked their view. He sped up until they came to the Gates property next door. "Maybe Big Roy will add it to his compound. He's already got Carin's and…"

"HANK, STOP!" Tippi cried out. She threw her arm across Hank's chest.

"Jesus, Mary and Joseph! You almost gave me a heart attack. What the hell's the matter with you?"

"Back up, back up." She bounced in her seat and reached for the steering wheel.

"Tabitha…"

"I think I saw somebody walking up the driveway."

FORTY-FOUR

Norman Seitz held the Ruger in his right hand and stepped off the narrow gravel drive into the relative cover of the honeysuckle and over-grown brush that ran alongside the Gates' driveway. He pushed his way forward.

As the house came into view, Norm paused to catch his breath and to figure out what to do next. He was prepared to kill Big Roy. But, he wondered, what about Velma? Could he bring himself to shoot a woman, even if the woman looked like a hotdog wrapped in dough and smelled like bacon and gym socks? He didn't think so. On the other hand, he couldn't leave any witnesses; he'd put a bullet in his own brain before he'd go to prison.

He did a visual survey of the layout in front of him. The house lay to the left, obscured by a hedge that hadn't seen pruning shears in years. A bay window peeked out over the bushes. *Maybe I could bust that window, burst through and scare 'em to death.*

An old adage from his training in sales, *Keep It Simple Stupid,* came to mind. He tightened his grip on the gun and stepped onto the walk that led to the front door.

Norm waited. He'd rung the doorbell, knocked and called out to Big Roy to 'open the damn door'. He walked around to the back of the house to a cement slab that served as a patio. A rusted-out table and some lawn chairs with bowed frames and frayed webbing comprised the owners' attempts at outdoor furnishings. Several ashtrays overflowing with cigarette butts and cigar stubs added to the ambiance.

Norm peered through the filthy glass window that opened to the kitchen. He considered breaking the glass with the butt of his gun when he felt something cold and wet brush against his hand. He swung around and aimed the gun. It was Moose, the Gates' dog. When his heart eventually slowed and he caught his breath, he squatted down and patted the animal's head.

"Jeez, you shouldn't sneak up on a man with a gun, you stupid mutt." He kneaded the animal's ears. "You're the one member of this family that deserves to live." He took the dog's face in his hands. He dodged the long red tongue aiming for his lips. "Where is everybody, Moose? They leave you all alone to guard the place?" He chuckled. "You're big alright but not very bright. Guess that's what makes you a Gates."

Moose, the canine version of the animal from which he got his name, turned over onto on his back beside Norm and nosed the man's hand. "Belly rub, huh? You're a real tough guy." Norm absently stroked the animal while he sized up the situation. His gaze swept the back of the house for signs of life when he noticed something at the base of the door. "What do we have here?" He holstered his gun and took a closer look. He ran his fingers around a frame that supported a piece of heavy plastic painted the same color as the door. Norm guessed the opening to be at least two feet high and almost that wide. The animal nudged Norm aside and squeezed through. From inside, he barked an invitation for Norm to come in.

Moose licked Norm's face as the man wriggled and panted and squeezed through the flap. Once inside, he stood up, brushed himself off and inspected the rip on his sleeve where he'd caught it on the hinge. "You owe me a shirt, buddy. I'll..." Norm jumped and drew out his gun; voices came from the next room. He pulled the slide back and chambered a round. He flattened himself against the wall and edged his way to the corner where he was able to get a good visual of the room's interior. From his vantage point, he could see a vintage style radio atop a stack of books beside a worn out sofa, the only piece of furniture in the room. A light from the radio indicated it was on and appeared to be the source of the voices. Still, to be on the safe side, he called out, "Hello? Anybody there?" before he went in.

Gripping the gun, Norm scowled at the sofa blanketed in dog hair, shrugged, and sat down. "What do they say, Moose? Lay down with dogs, wake up with fleas?" He stroked the dog's head with the muzzle of the Ruger. "Okay, buddy, what's plan B? I didn't expect there'd be a need." He looked around the dusty room. "Now—wait a second—hold that thought. What's this?" Loose wires hung from the middle of the long wall across from where he was seated. He got up to get a closer look when he spotted a cable box partially hidden behind a pile of discarded pizza boxes and a trash can filled with empty beer cans. "Looks like somebody had a party, And," he mused, "from what I know about your momma, I'd say she either had enough of Big Roy and took her TV and left, or," he studied marks in the carpet from where a heavy object had been dragged across the floor, "the whole motley crew—apologies, my man—took a powder and left me—and you, I might add—high and dry."

Norm cocked his head. *Was that a vehicle coming up the drive?* He looked out the bay window. Nothing. "Guess I'm a little jumpy, buddy." Norm followed Moose back into the kitchen. The animal shuffled to a corner of the room where two cylindrical towers sat, one held water, the other food. Both were full. Moose nosed a lever releasing water into a dish below. He repeated the procedure with the food container. "So, are they coming back or not?" Norm opened the refrigerator. Empty, except for a single can of Mountain Dew. He took it out and checked the freezer—it was full. "Hmm, that's weird. If they weren't coming back, they'd have emptied the freezer." Moose trotted to the front door and barked. "Right," Norm said, engrossed in his own thoughts. "And I know they would've left their kids before they left you. I don't get it."

He opened the soda then checked the cupboards for Big's stash of Jack Daniels. In the far corner of an otherwise empty cabinet was a single bottle with barely enough liquor for one stiff drink. "That proves one thing, Moose," he said, looking around for the dog, "Big Roy is sure not coming back. He took all his booze."

Norm took a tumbler from one of the cupboards and sat down at the kitchen table. He emptied the liquor into the glass. "Wouldn't it be a hoot," he called to the dog who had planted his big body by the front door, "if I rented the place out?" He twirled the Ruger on the tabletop as he spoke. "I'd love to see Big Roy's face when he came home to find…"

Moose whimpered from the other room.

"Moose?'

Norm grabbed his gun and ran into the living room. Smiling at him across the room was Deputy Moira Potts, her service revolver pointed at his chest. Moose lay in the corner drooling over a turkey sandwich, the remnants of Moira's lunch.

Norm stepped back. He fixed his weapon on Moira.

"Norm? Don't be stupid. We just need to talk."

Norm snickered.

Moira tightened her grip on the revolver. *Steady, girl.*

Norm spread his feet and moved the gun muzzle to rest against his temple. "What's next, deputy? I can't go to prison and I've got nothing to live for." He breathed hard. "So, who's gonna do the honors? You—or…?"

Out of the corner of his eye, he saw a shadow move through the open door. Startled, he dropped the hand holding the gun.

Moira dove forward. She knocked Norm to the floor, the Ruger firing as they landed. She felt a sharp pain in her side. "You shot me, you stupid…" She moved her hand to her rib expecting to find blood. Instead, something hard jammed into her side. "What?"

She lifted her head. Tippi Mulgrew stood over her, the plastic boot in Moira's side, the silver whistle in her mouth.

Phsst

FORTY-FIVE

"Sheriff," a deputy called from across the room. He held up a silver bag he'd discovered at the rear of one of the drawers in the file cabinet.

Grange made his way through the cluster of technicians and officers crowding Norm's office. Norm's car had been found across the street from Fowler Tower and was being towed to the station.

"Funny place to store coffee, don't you think?" the officer said.

Grange held out a gloved hand and examined the bag. "I've seen this before," he said. "Right before I wound up in the hospital."

The deputy raised his eyebrows.

Grange's stomach lurched remembering that night at the Alvarezes and pulling into his garage before everything went dark. "I'll ask BCI to put a rush on this. Thanks, Deputy, good catch."

Another officer approached Grange. "We've gone through the files in the desk and boxed 'em up, Sheriff. We also pulled some stuff out of the trash you might want to look at."

The empty drawers hung open; the top of the desk was littered with paper, creased from where it had been crumpled up and tossed away. The sheriff smoothed out the creases on one of the papers, a certificate embossed with some sort of seal and emblazoned with the name Fowler University College of Realtors across the top. Another document was a promissory note between Norm and Bobo Fowler that showed Norman Seitz had promised to pay F.U.C.R. forty thousand dollars for tuition. *Paid In Full* was scrawled across the page. The black imprint of a man's shoe blurred the signatures.

Grange handed the documents back. "Bag 'em up," he instructed the officer. "And what have we here?" The sheriff plucked a pen matching the one found at Bobo's from the detritus on the desktop. "And who says it's not Christmas?" He turned the pen over to a waiting technician.

Grange stood a moment to watch the teams methodically and professionally conduct their search before stepping into the hall. "I'll be at the station if anybody needs me," he told the officer stationed by the front door. "BCI will take what they need to the lab. Tell the guys to bring everything else uptown." He shook the deputy's hand and headed for the parking lot. He was about to call his sergeant when his cellphone rang. "Hey, Ed. I was just about to …what? Are you kidding? Well, we can call off the search for 'im, anyway. Good news, for a change, right? I'll head right over there. Anything else I should know?" As he listened, he pushed his hat to the back of his head and rubbed his eyes.

"How in blazes did she manage that?"

...

The faded sofa cushions sagged under the weight of Norman

Seitz squeezed between Tippi Mulgrew and Hank Klaber. Only Norm was handcuffed, although Moira let it be known if she'd had two more pairs of cuffs she'd have used them on Tippi and Hank too. Deputy Potts scowled and paced in front of the trio and fought a losing battle to hold her temper.

"What on God's green earth were you thinking?" she exploded at Hank. "I get it that…that your *girlfriend*," Moira spit out the words, "doesn't have the sense God gave a goose, but you, Hank?" She shook her head and alternately glared at Hank, then at Tippi.

Hank shrugged. He couldn't think of a single excuse to justify the fact that he had caved in to Tippi's demand that they follow Moira when the deputy arrived at the Gates'. He'd reminded her that when they called the station about sighting a person that looked like Norm at Big Roy's place, Ed warned them in no uncertain terms to 'get the hell out of there and stay away'. Hank knew he was 'spittin' in the wind' as Grange often liked to say, so he'd agreed they would follow Moira at a safe distance when she drove up Bobo's driveway and took the path that connected Fowler's property to Gates'. He'd made Tippi wait until Moira was out of sight before he helped her out of the car and along the path leading to Big Roy's yard. They stood back, hidden in the trees while they watched the deputy go inside before they went up to the house. The rest—that was all Tippi.

FORTY-SIX

The members of the Goose Down Senior Citizens' Center were preparing to celebrate the weddings of Elrod and Wittekind. Tippi supervised Amy and Carin as they put the final touches on the white and pink crepe-paper streamers and tissue paper wedding bells along the walls. Hank and Sheriff Grange placed chairs around tables festooned in crisp white tablecloths and bowls of fresh pink and white carnations. Kegs of beer had been tapped and buffet tables were loaded with offerings from Olive Garden, commemorating the happy couples' first date. A six-tiered wedding cake decorated in pink and white, with sparklers placed around the base, towered on a cart in the kitchen.

Hank stood back to admire his handiwork when he was joined by Grange, Applebee and Perry, of The One Man Band, who'd offered to help set up.

"Looks good," Perry said.

"Yeah," Hank agreed, wiping beads of sweat from his forehead.

"Oh, oh," Applebee said, "Here comes the boss."

Tippi barreled across the room as fast as she was able in her new pink ballet flats. She'd told Dr. Schneider that she had to have "this damn plastic contraption off once and for all" referring to the brace she'd been wearing since her release from the hospital. She'd explained she needed to buy some shoes that didn't look like something only a nun or a hundred year old man would wear, since she planned to dance at her friends' wedding.

"You look very nice, Tippi," Applebee said. "You match the decorations."

"I know." Tippi pirouetted, the pale pink chiffon of her long skirt floated around her. The bodice of pink and white sequins matched the headband struggling to corral her pink and gray curls.

Perry leaned toward her chest to get a closer look at the flash of silver he'd spotted around her neck. "What's that?" he asked, reaching out.

"Back off band man or you'll be playing that accordion with your feet." Tippi made a grab for his fingers before they reached the silver chain.

"Tippi, take that off," Hank said sternly. "This is neither the time nor the place."

Tippi responded by reaching into her bosom and bringing out her whistle. *Pssssht*, she blew hard enough that the men backed up and covered their ears.

"Tabitha, I demand that you remove that thing for the remainder of the evening." Hank held out his hand and wriggled his fingers. "It—and you—caused more than your share of trouble. Now, hand the damn thing over."

"And if I refuse?" Tippi said.

The men moved behind Hank.

"If you refuse, you will be looking for another dance partner, if you get my drift," Hank said matter-of-factly. His upturned hand was as steady as his stare into the eyes of the woman whose antics could have gotten one, or both, of them, killed. Lucky for them, the sheriff had persuaded his deputy not to follow through on her insistence that Hank and Tippi be charged with obstructing justice.

Tippi held onto the whistle and tapped her fingers against her breast while she returned Hank's gaze. Finally, she slipped the chain over her head, handed it over and twirled away.

...

Hank stood with his plate of food searching the room for somewhere to sit away from the revelers and another rendition of *Roll Out The Barrel*. He watched Tippi directing the women to form a dance circle around the brides who blushed and laughed and held one another's hands as they were ushered into the center of the ring.

"I brought my own seat," Applebee joked, rolling up beside Hank with a full plate on his lap. "What do you say we find a table out of the way and you get us a pitcher of beer?" He smiled across the room at the party in full swing. Tonight, it was time to celebrate.

"Not dancing?" Carin asked as she joined them.

"Left my dancing shoes at home," Applebee said, straight-faced.

"What about you?" Hank asked, putting an arm around Carin's waist.

"No. As soon as they cut the cake, I have to go."

"Oh?" Hank looked at Applebee, who raised his shoulders.

"Sauerkraut and I are taking the Harley and getting away for awhile. We're leaving tomorrow on a ride that will take us though the Rockies and eventually to Yosemite. I haven't figured out what I'll do after that. Maybe just hang out until my divorce is final and then," she shrugged, "who knows?"

"Wow, I had no idea," Applebee said.

"That's terrific, I'm really impressed." Hank said. "If you want, I can check on your place while you're gone, water plants…"

"Eat your food," Applebee added.

"Thank you, but I've asked Victor and Arcella to move in for the time being. They need somewhere to live and I'll feel better knowing they're taking care of everything."

"And *being* taken care of, I'll wager," Applebee said.

"Over here, guys," Wittekind called to the threesome. "We're getting ready to cut the cake."

"Before we do the honors," Elrod announced, as everyone gathered around, "let's hear it for Arcella who created this masterpiece, and for Victor who managed to get it here in one piece."

"Thank you," Victor said, his arm tight around his wife. "Thank you for believing in us." He rested moist eyes on Carin, "Next week, we will become citizens of this great country."

The guests roared and clapped their approval while the Alvarezes looked embarrassed and pleased.

"Ready to roll?" Hank asked Applebee after snagging two generous slices of cake.

"Should we invite those characters to join us?" Applebee

nodded to Wittekind and Elrod who stood with Grange looking lost after posing for pictures pushing cake into their brides' mouths. "The bridegrooms look like they could use a break."

...

Elrod leaned back in his chair and patted his paunch. He wiped frosting from his upper lip and licked his finger. "Man, that was good. I'm ready for another slice."

"Better eat up now, buddy, 'cause your *wife* is gonna make sure you never enjoy another carb as long as you live," Wittekind joked.

"You should talk," Applebee told Wittekind. "That's why Frenchie is the only girl I let boss me around. We eat whatever and whenever..."

"But, does she keep your feet warm in bed at night?" Hank kidded.

"Matter of fact she does," Applebee said. He glanced at Grange who sat staring at his untouched food. "Something wrong, sheriff?" Applebee asked. "Not hungry?"

Grange looked up, startled. "Oh, no. Sorry guys. Just letting my mind wander."

"Care to tell us about it?" Applebee asked.

Grange gave Elrod and Wittekind a weak smile. "It's nothing. Like Amy says, I obsess about stuff. Besides," he held up his glass of beer that had grown warm, "tonight's for celebrating. Here's to Elrod and Wittekind, two lucky guys who proved there's no age limit on love."

"Hear, hear," Hank and Applebee chimed in.

Elrod beamed at his buddy. "Think we ought to get back?"

"I sure do," Wittekind said, rising. "I want to slow dance with my wife."

Elrod rolled his eyes and started for the door. "You guys coming?" he asked the others.

"We'll be out in a sec," said Hank. He waited until the two were gone before he spoke, "Okay, Pete, tell us what's bothering you."

"Problems with Amy?" Applebee asked.

"Oh, no," Grange said. "We're great." His face broke into a huge smile. "In fact," he lowered his voice and checked over his shoulder, "I popped the question last night. We didn't want to say anything to take away from Elrod and Wittekind's day, but," he dropped his voice to a whisper, "we're going down to the courthouse next week and make it official."

"That's great," Applebee said, clapping his friend's shoulder.

"Congratulations, Pete," Hank added. "I'm really happy for you both."

"Marriage is in the air, Hank," Applebee winked at his long time friend.

"Can't say the subject hasn't come up," Hank said.

"You got cold feet?" Applebee said.

"Not me. I would have done it before this. It's Tippi who isn't sure."

"About you? I can't believe it," Applebee said.

"She wants us to live together," Hank said. "And, I'm not sure how I feel about that."

"Old-fashioned, are you?" Applebee said.

"Guys?" Grange interrupted, "can I run something by you?"

Hank and Applebee exchanged glances. "Sorry, Pete. Of

course," Applebee said.

Grange waved his hand. "It's okay." He fidgeted with his fork and set his plate aside. "It's about the case."

"I can't shake the feeling that I missed something. I know the evidence pointed to Seitz, and Lord knows he crossed enough lines to get him put away for a long time but..." He looked up, his face grave.

Applebee and Hank waited.

"I mean, the guy's a scam artist, but a *killer*?" Grange shook his head and stared at his clenched fists.

"Pete, I know you and I know you left no stone unturned in this investigation," Applebee said.

"I agree," Hank said. "After all, Norm *told* Tippi he wanted to kill Bobo and Roy and then showed up at Big Roy's with the same gun that killed Bobo."

Applebee added, "Besides all that evidence you found in his office including the tainted coffee like what was at the center."

"That killed Gert," Hank said. "And Violet, not to mention all the people who got sick, including you, Pete." He could feel the heat spreading across his face when he thought of almost losing Tippi.

"Wittekind and Elrod are lucky they only lost their insurance," Applebee added.

"What do you always say, Pete? Motive, means and opportunity. The guy had all his hands all over this, literally," Hank said.

Grange nodded. "It's just..." he hesitated, "This goes no further, but it's Big Roy. We checked him out from every conceivable angle and couldn't find one iota of hard evidence to connect him to any of these deaths. His only crime, and it wasn't in the legal sense, was acting as a scout for Norm. We had only Norm's word that Roy was a full-fledged partner in the business and knew exactly what the score was." He took a swallow of beer. "My hunch is that he probably was, I just couldn't prove it."

"I've always viewed Roy as a wily old coot who's only interested in making an easy buck. He made a bundle from his deal, I should say, deals, with CLAW," Hank opined.

"Don't forget what he made off Leon," Applebee said.

Grange nodded. "That was the one move where I almost nailed him. But when the staff from SunDown Ridge testified Roy had been Leon's only visitor for months leading up to his death and testified when Norm did show up, he let everyone know he was counting the days until Leon passed..."

A pall, like a gray shroud, fell over the men.

The sheriff set his empty glass on the floor next to his chair. "Remember when I put Roy on the stand, sitting there hooked up to that tank of oxygen looking for all the world like some frail old codger, how he managed to convince the jury that he was just another one of Norm's victims? Almost had me convinced too."

"Almost?" Applebee asked.

Finally, Hank spoke again, "Now, I'm no expert, but I know you, Pete, and you are as thorough a man as I ever met. If Roy was involved, you would have found it."

The sheriff's face fell. "Gert and Violet deserved justice. I only hope they got it."

FORTY-SEVEN

Big Roy sat on the lanai of his brand new patio home. A deep tan had replaced his normally pasty complexion so that Royal Gates almost looked like a healthy—and happy—man. Roy's attention alternated between admiring the new BMW golf cart parked in his driveway and re-reading an article in the Cincinnati Enquirer about Donald Harvey, the most infamous serial killer in America. Dubbed the Angel-of-Death, his victims were mostly poor and elderly, in hospitals and nursing homes throughout the greater Cincinnati area. Harvey had bragged about the fact that he'd killed more people than Ted Bundy and had escaped justice many years before he was finally apprehended. The newspaper reported that after nearly thirty years in prison, he was dead of injuries sustained in an attack from a fellow inmate.

Roy folded up the paper and turned to his wife. "I wonder if I brought that book about Harvey with me. You know, he actually autographed it. I'd like to keep it but it might be worth some money on eBay."

"Don't know," Velma said. She was lying in a hammock reading *The National Enquirer.* She swung one pudgy leg over the side in a futile attempt to touch the floor. "Gimme a push."

Big Roy stretched out his long leg and shoved.

"Big?"

"Hmmm."

"Why'd it take us so long to realize Florida is where we belong?" She looked pensive. "Wish we'd made the move sooner."

"We didn't have the dough."

"Gotta admit, Big, this is living." Velma had dived in to their new lifestyle with both freshly pedicured feet. Today she was wearing one of her new muumuus. She'd told her husband she never knew a woman could be so comfortable *and* so stylish at the same time, so she bought a dozen of the dresses festooned with brightly colored flowers and birds. She came home one day, arms loaded with shopping bags, wearing one of the new creations. The fabric was festooned with psychedelic swirls and curls that ballooned from Velma's shoulders to the tops of her red sandals. As she twirled around the room, arms outstretched, the dress and the flab from her arms rippled as she spun. She looked like some exotic, South American fowl taxiing for take off and as she whirled, she trilled, "Big, I feel just like a bird let out of a cage and I'll tell you one thing for sure, I ain't never going back." Then she declared she was ditching all of her bras.

Big Roy gave his wife one last push in the hammock and turned back to his paper when his cellphone rang.

"That another salesman?" Velma asked. "Tell 'em we ain't interested." Since the couple had arrived at The Villages, they'd been besieged with calls from salespeople hawking everything from termite inspections to burial plots. Big Roy liked to string them along for entertainment and to satisfy his ornery streak.

"It's Baby," he sighed. "What's up, boy?" As he listened, his face broke into a big smile. "Well, isn't that a hoot? Glad to hear he's making the most of his situation. He never was one to let the grass grow under his feet." Big cackled. "I'll tell your ma. You all take it easy, hear?"

Velma waited for Roy to fill her in.

"Baby says, 'Hey'." He paused. He knew Velma was itching to know what their youngest had called about.

Velma squirmed into a sitting position. "Yeah, and what else?" she barked.

"Milty's fine." Big Roy scratched the new growth on his chin. He'd decided to give up shaving since he was now a man of leisure and had better things to do, like drive the golf cart around the neighborhood or watch the landscape crew mow his grass.

"Still waitin', Big," Velma said. She pumped her legs to make the hammock swing.

"Norman Seitz," Big said. He shook his head and grinned. "He's got himself a new, little business."

Velma stopped pumping. "What? A business? Did those fools let 'im out?"

"No, woman. He calls Warren Correctional home now. He's not going anywhere—at least for a while."

"Too bad he'll be eligible for parole someday."

"Yeah, but you'll be long gone."

"More likely you'll be the one that's…"

"Yeah, yeah, I hear you, old woman." Big Roy looked thoughtful but that passed. "At least Norm didn't pull off an OJ.

Fact that Gert and Violet's deaths were based on circumstantial evidence could have meant reasonable doubt and he would've skated. Lucky they nailed him as the guy who killed Fowler."

"'And the stuff about cheatin' old people and newlyweds."

"Yeah." Big studied his new diamond signet ring. "There is that."

Velma stopped swinging and looked downcast. "I been wondering Big—do you think he actually poisoned the people at the center that day at the tournament? I wish we knew for sure. Gert and me had our spats but I always thought of her as a friend and I think she felt the same about me." She blew her nose in the hanky she dug out the folds of her dress.

Big stared hard at his wife, his brow furrowed. It was a full minute before he spoke. "Gert was a decent woman, Velma, and I am sorry she died. Violet too." He pursed his lips. "Don't forget though, Seitz was in cahoots with Fowler to sell Ernie's land so naturally he had to get both him and Gert out of the way. Violet just happened to be in the wrong place at the wrong time. And," he added, "Grange found the poisoned coffee squirreled away in a file cabinet in Seitz' office."

"What? Where'd you hear that, Big? I never read that nowhere." Velma's forehead creased in a frown.

Roy leaned forward, his face reddening under his tan. "It was on the news, woman. Maybe if you stopped reading this crap," he yanked the *Enquirer* off his wife's lap, his voice hard, "and tried *real* news..." He balled up the paper and hurled it across the room. "And, of course," he went on, choosing his words carefully, "there was that other *small* matter of Seitz showing up at our place with a gun to *kill me*." Big Roy's look shot daggers at his wife.

"I know, Big. That woulda been awful."

"Well, for me, anyway," Roy said. "You know, Vel, he mighta killed you too, then got our place for a song if those dumbass kids..."

Velma switched gears. "Yeah, Big," she interjected, "you're probably right."

Roy didn't like the *probably* in that sentence but decided to let it go. He'd been trying hard to bury the past. Most of the time it worked. And besides, except for the Schwabs and Violet, Bobo had what happened to him coming and as far as Big thought, the world was a much better place for it.

His wife was somber for a minute, then brightened. "What kinda business is Norm into? Funny business?" She laughed at her own joke.

Big relaxed. "It is pretty funny, Vel. He cornered the market on the prison's hot chocolate concession."

"Huh?" Velma studied her newly manicured nails, each one embellished with a different glittery flower.

"Right off the bat, after he learned the lay of the land, he started using the small amount of money in his account at the prison commissary to buy up all the hot chocolate they had." Big studied the cover of his book. "You know, those little packets you add to water? Seems criminals love the stuff. So, he buys 'em all up, sells them back to the inmates, and pockets the profits." Big yawned and stretched. "Right outta the Bernie Madoff playbook. Gotta hand it to Norm, he always could figure out how to make lemonade."

"Humph, can't be much money in hot chocolate."

"I dunno, but of course he don't need much. The State of Ohio's covering his room, board, health and dental. And they give him a fancy orange suit and a haircut every month." Big Roy ran his hand through his own thinning hair.

The couple sat quietly. Finally, Velma broke the silence and asked, "You ever have any regrets, Big? I mean, 'bout—stuff?"

"Way I see it, Vel, we was only lookin' out for our own selves—and our kids. Nobody else in that hick town gave a tinker's damn about you *or* me and Lord knows all three of them kids together don't have the brains God gave a goose." He opened his book. "And as for Norm, why, the guy was, as they say, 'a danger to himself and *others*'. So, everything we did was for the greater good. We're like—social workers."

Velma nodded. She swung her legs back into the hammock and sank deep into the mesh folds.

Big Roy's cellphone chimed an incoming text message from *Unknown Caller*. He swiped the green icon and watched as a picture uploaded, immediately followed by a second. "What the …?" He frowned and looked closer. A screenshot showed Big sitting at Bobo Fowler's desk, the Ruger in his hand clearly visible. A second image showed the three Gates offspring clustered around their father next to Bobo's Mercedes, Baby Roy high-fiving GG, still dressed in her white coveralls.

ABOUT THE AUTHOR

The author is a former geriatric social worker living in southwestern Ohio with her husband. Witte's experiences with older adults and life in a rural community have provided the inspiration for her work.

Other books by the author are, *Bingo-You're Dead (Volume 1, Murder Is My Game) and M$. Fortune: Fifty Shades of Gray, as author, Kandy Witte.* All are available on Amazon.

www.ingramcontent.com/pod-product-compliance
Lightning Source LLC
Chambersburg PA
CBHW071127170626
46809CB00002B/520